Karma

AFoxxyDProduction

A NOVEL

WRITTEN BY

Destiny Cook

Acknowledgements

First and foremost I would like to give honor to the man above. Secondly, I would like to thank my family and friends who stood by me throughout my madness, reading my short stories and encouraging me to turn them into a book. To every person who messaged me asking me for the next story and the next chapter, this is for you.

To anyone who feels like their dreams are too far fetched or unattainable. Never give up, don't allow your finances or any circumstances stop you from making it happen. I wrote this book on my cellphone. I'm just a South-Central girl by way of Century Blvd & Western Ave getting it done.

Welcome to a FoxxyD Production

Table of Contents

Chapter 1
Makenzie Gray

♫ *"Nigga I don't give a fuck.*
Ride with my niggas
Like fuck it, die with my niggas
You a nigga with bitch ways
You remind me of my bitch name, Tiffany. ♫

YG bumping by my friends out of my blueberry Honda Civic coupe, as clouds of smoke escape the cars hot-boxing around us. It was the dead of night, but the night was still young. Nobody in their right minds was out, but us crazy college kids eager to get to the next party. The temperature was what felt like below zero. But in reality, it was only about fifty degrees. This type of temperature was freezing conditions to an LA chick like me. Trust and believe cold weather didn't stop me from dressing like a hot girl, and acting out in true saddity nature, ready to be on the scene.

As I strut towards my car, swaying my hips to my natural rhythm to show off my curvy figure. I was that chick, and you couldn't tell me a damn thing. My outfit was party girl certified for the night. I was rocking a black crop top two-piece set with flared bottoms hugging my butt in all the right places. Body adorned with gold like a true queen, wearing a gold rope chain with a name charm, a Rolex choker, some twisty hoops, bust down with my gleaming Michael Kors watch and strappy sandals tied around my ankle. My hair was the bomb with my recently installed curly bundles bouncing in the air as my natural face shined radiantly accenting my glossy pout lips.

Suddenly, a black Kia Forte darts straight towards my direction, almost taking me out. As I hopped out of the way and tried to look and see who it was, I heard the girls talking shit in the car.

"Yeah, that bitch better had moved out the way." Followed by the cackling of the hyenas sitting in the passenger seats.

"Exactly, fuck it, hit that bitch." My eyes went on high alert to see who the bitches in this car were. I know that voice from somewhere, that's for damn sure. My body immediately began to tense, as I caught sight of Parker sitting in the driver seat. Oh, she picked the right one to fuck with today. I had my bitches with me tonight, so it was nothing to run this much-needed fade.

"GET OUT THE CAR THEN BITCH!" I scream, moving my curly hair from sticking on my glossy lips.

"YOU WANNA BE BAD!? GET OUT THE MUTHA-FUCKIN WHIP! WHAT'S GOOD?" Hip popped out to one side with both hands on my hips, waiting for her to get out of the car.

Skuuuuuurrttttttt!

She zoomed out of the packed Lucky's grocery parking lot that sat directly across from the last party at the Long Beach Men's' volleyball team house. I hurried to my car ready to catch her at the next function. I was not even paying attention to the massive crowd looking around at me like a lunatic, trying to square up with five bitches in a car.

"Let's go yall we outta here. I'm about to beat her fucking ass. She just tried to hit me with the fucking whip!" As I shuffled anxiously, trying to turn on the ignition to my car.

"Wait, what happened, where she at?" Said Kiani, as she looked at me in a chill but concerned tone.

No matter the circumstances, my girl Kiani was always so damn calm about shit. But right now wasn't the time for no explanation. My stomach was balled in a million knots, and my hands were sweating. I needed to get out of this parking lot and whoop some ass. I was ready for whatever the rest of the night had in store.

"They on their way to the basketball house, let's gooooooo" I nagged.

"Girl, wait a minute, let me put on my seat belt." Miranda was surprising always down with my missions even though she was quite snobbish.

All six of us adjust in my blueberry civic coupe. Kiani, Carissa, and the homeboys Aj and Riley all packed in the back seat with Miranda and me in the front.

I start the car up, back out quickly and... **BOOM**

I back right into somebody white beetle. Everybody on looking and talking their talk

"Damnnnnn she ran right into her shit!"

"Oh shit, are they about to fight?"

A thin curly hair, fair complexion girl angrily gets out of the car. She stands there, looks at her car, and stares blankly at me. Our cars are now damn near bumper to bumper with a couple of inches in between for me to assess the damages.

"So, do you want to exchange information?" I say in a confused voice as she stands there with no reply.

It was like she was one of those impressionable bitches, waiting for the crowd to tell her what to do. At this point, I had somewhere to be, and she needed to hurry this shit up.

"Girl, what do you wanna do? Wassup? You want my information or what?"

No reply.

"You know what, fuck it we outta here yall let's go," I say as I walk back to the driver seat of my car.

"Girl, you get in the passenger side, you hitting people's car and shit," Kiani says, snatching the keys out of my hand and getting in the driver seat.

Kiani has been driving us around the city before any of us was old enough to have a license anyway. So, I obliged.

"Aye, take me home first y'all I can't go," Riley said scrunched up in the back seat with Carissa in his lap.

I guess the idea of riding smashed in the back seat to a chick fight wasn't that appealing to him.

⚓

We parked outside the "The Basketball House," which technically wasn't a house at all, just the apartment building that the Long Beach Mens' basketball team lived. We parked on the dark street right in front of the apartment, waiting to see Parker and her group of friends pull up to the party. Ten minutes had passed, and we saw a jam-packed black Kia Forte drive pass the front of the apartment blasting some Problem.

"Alright, let's give them some time to park and get settled at the party. Then we gonna go up in there." I pulled my curly weave up in a low ponytail. I took all my jewelry off, placing it in my cup holder, and got my gold glitter Ugg boots out of the trunk and put them on. I was ready for my fade.

"Y'all ready? Let's go." I stare at all of them blankly.

I know damn well they not gonna let me go into a party of bitches for a fade by myself. Miranda and Carissa get out of the car. AJ had got comfortable in the back seat, finally given some leg room since Riley was dropped off and Carissa and Miranda got out of the car.

"Naw, I'm chilling, imma wait in the car until y'all come back," Aj says stretching out.

"Yeah, I'm with Aj, going to sit here too so when y'all come back we can drive off," Kiani says, reapplying her lip gloss before taking a selfie with her phone.

Kiani has never been a fighter, but she was one hell of a speed racer. So, I wasn't tripping.

Carissa, Miranda and I crept through the main building gates.

"Do yall know what the apartment number is?" Carissa whispered, trying not to catch the attention of the security patrolling the building.

"Girl, I don't know, I know how to get there. So, follow me." Miranda didn't say a word; she just followed my lead with a tense look on her face like she didn't know what was coming next.

We made it to the apartment door. And no bullshit it was like everything was an out-of-body experience. This was it, now or never. Was this shit worth fighting over? I thought to myself about all the prior encounters Parker and I have had. I've spotted her coming out of my boyfriend Jeremy's dorm room. I even found her greasy what she claimed to be "Pauline's" hair in the sheets and her panties under his bed.

I thought about the last big dispute we had over Twitter this past Christmas break, starting rumors about me saying I slept with dusty as Pete at a Squad party. I told that bird brain hoe then, next time we have an issue. I was done talking, and be ready to line it up period. Cause I need my issue. This Long Beach bitch doesn't even know how we LA girls do it, and she was gonna find out tonight.

THUMP THUMP THUMP

It was like a ghost that opened the door to a dark cave. And as we walked in, whatever doubts I had going on through my mind on if I wanted to fight was out the window. I looked at my girls. "Let's get it."

Chapter 2
Jeremy McCall

"Ohhhh! don't stop Mac I'm coming."

"Ahhhhhh shit ... You coming, huh?"

"Yeah ... right there baby... ahhh."

We both climaxed together as she collapsed on her stomach from the doggy style position I had her in. Shit, I'm feeling great right about now, all I need is a fat ass blunt.

"Taylooooor!" I yell playfully as I caress her fat ass, damn near in a daze looking at the butterfly tattoo she has on her whole right cheek. "Take me to the med shop up the street so that we can smoke."

⅏

Nipsey Hussle 'A Million' blasting in her black 328i 3 series BMW as we smoke at Whaley Park across the street from campus dorms. I rapped every lyric word for word.

♫ "I got my mind on a million 'fore I turn 26.
But that's just what it costs for that condo at the Ritz
I got this European belt, belt, European bitch
Ever seen an African in a European whip?" ♫

Thick clouds of smoke fill the car with every exhale.

"Bae, you staying here with me tonight?" I ask, eyes low from this Obama kush. I take another hit.

"Nah, not tonight Mac, you forgot I have work at 4 am?"

"Maaaaaaan, fuck that job when I get on you're not going to have to work another day in your life," I say smoothly as I give a quick brush to my dipping fade.

"Yeah yeah, well until then... I'm taking my ass to this hospital for my shift." She says playfully giving a grab to my dick and kissing seductively on my lips. She got me on the go again by sucking my bottom lip. She's a fucking freak.

Taylor was my main girl, she been around since high school and ain't nothing gonna change about that. When my mom got sick last semester, she was right in the hospital with me day in and day out checking on her making sure she straight.

I mean yeah, I'm fucking with a couple of girls on campus, but it's my freshman year of college. I mean ain't that what college is all about? Meeting new friends, hanging with the homies, and fucking bitchessssss. Ha!

Aye, don't get me wrong, I ain't anybody's dog. Taylor and I are not even together right now. But y'all know how that shit goes, that's all me.

"Alright, bae I'll see you later, get out the car and give me another kiss and stop playing."

"Maaaaccc, I gotta go," she nagged as she got out the car wrapping her arms around my neck. Placing one big fat wet kiss on her pink plump lips, and then annoyingly placing kisses all over her cheeks and forehead.

"Ughhhhh ha ha ha, you and these big ole wet kisses like a damn puppy." She knows she liked this shit.

"You know I love you. You mine"

"Yes, boy, I know... shit, you better love me!" She says as she hopped back in the car, but not before giving my dick another quick grab.

"You better stop playing with me girl before you be calling off from work tomorrow!" I give my waves another brush and re-adjust my basketball shorts and head back to my dorm room.

It's a late Saturday night; the halls of the dorm were quiet. They probably were quiet because everybody was out at those bullshit college parties. Not even really my scene like that I'm more of a low-key type of nigga. Plus, Makenzie, Parker and a couple of chicks I had in my company all been going out every weekend. Fuck that, wasn't gonna have me caught up.

I make it to my empty dorm room, grateful that my roommate, Vin, goes home every weekend. I hopped in the shower, changed out my sheets, and cut on Archer until I drifted off to deep sleep. Good pussy will drain you like that.

Bzzzzzzzz Bzzzzzzzz Bzzzzzzz

It's 2 o'clock in the morning and Makenzie calling....

"Hello... was-sup?" I answer restlessly...

"Hello? Macc can you hear me?!" Makenzie says anxiously. Damn, why this girl got so much energy this late.

"Yeah I can, what's going on. You straight?"

"Baby!" She screams in her little southern belle tone.

"Parker tried to hit me with her car at the Volleyball house! I met her up at the Basketball party and whooped her ass. I don't know what she thought! She was fucking with the wrong one!"

Makenzie, Makenzie, Makenzie... she was my firecracker. From the moment I met her, I knew I had a rider on my hands. Her little boughetto spunk to her made her even that more appealing.

"Baby, I broke my nail, hitting her. It hurts so badly... where are you at? I want to see you." She was so sexy with that sassy shit. But she thinks she slick huh? Trying to come over here after she started some shit.

"I'm in my room come through."

As we hang up, my phone is alarming with notifications.

DING

AJ: Aye bro shit went down tonight.

DING DING

Parker: Nigga! Because of you, this damn girl come hitting me in my fucking face!

Parker: Where the fuck are you anyway?!

DING

Colton: Brooooooooooooooo match tomorrow tonight was wild bruh! LOL

Mann. This was about to be some semester. But I promise you one thing. These females weren't gone force my hand to do anything. I sit up in bed; take my du-rag off gave my waves a quick brush and checked to make sure none of Taylor shit is in here for Makenzie to find.

My phone rings, its Makenzie.

"Hey, I'm outside your dorm, please open the door."

Man she playing, it's damn near 4 a.m; at this point, she's lucky I'm still up. I get to the C buildings door, and there she was. Hair braided up in two plats on the side with a silky black headscarf, a cheetah print short set, and some gold glitter UGGs. She has the face of a doll with her chocolate skin and deep dimples, but the attitude of a gangsta. She claimed to be a tough girl like she doesn't take any bull shit. But I know I got her. All that rah-rah sassy, tough girl shit she portrays is fake news to a nigga like Mac.

"So, you been a bad girl tonight I hear?" I say as I grab her around her waist, kissing her on her forehead.

"Oh hush up Mac... she made me break a nail look!" Makenzie says, showing me her broken nails.

I go in my wallet and throw 30 dollars on the desk in my room. Brushing my hair and putting back on my du-ag.

"Don't worry about that; I got you. Come on Kenz baby, let's go to bed."

Chapter 3
Miranda Beal

"Kenz always got me in some bullshit," I say to myself lifelessly as I finally plop into my bed to rest before I get up to pick my girlfriend Judith up from work. I was exhausted, but responsibilities didn't seem to care about how tired I was. Before I knew it, it was time to get up again.

"I need to get out of these clothes and take a shower." As I huff, bite the bullet and decide to get up and start getting ready for the rest of my day. I take a good look at my body after hopping out of the shower. I was less than pleased with this damn stomach. I have been working out three days a week, but it seemed like I was never going to get the insta-model shapes like my girls. I was a solidly built chick, not made for nobody tiny. Growing up, grown men use to call me a stallion and fawn over how mature my body was. But I didn't like all that attention and the guys, my age, all they wanted to do was to get in my panties. It wasn't until my first encounter with a female that someone tried to get to know me for who I was, and not just my body. I didn't feel used.

I un-wrapped my hair that fell into a blunt merlot color bob cut that cuffed at the dimples on my cheeks. I didn't play about my hair. If this body wasn't going to be how I wanted it to be; this hair was going to be everything and more. I wanted to be cute picking up Judith, so I put on a highlighter orange sundress that shined against my pale vanilla skin, it accentuated my thighs and unfortunately, showing off my little pudge, so I put on a destroyed denim jacket to cover it. I slipped on some black furry slides and grabbed my black MCM fanny-pack. I'm surprised I even have the energy to put effort into my appearance after leaving Makenzie's dorm, going straight to work and finally coming home.

After the other night, I don't know if I ever want to go to another school party again. It was crazy; I swear, somebody should write a book about it.

Oh yeah, that's what we're doing right now. Anyway, let me tell you guys what happened once Makenzie led us to the basketball house.

"So y'all not about to get out the car?" Kenz asked, looking at us like she was ready to fight us next. I mean I was going to get out the car regardless, but I didn't think she was going to be so pumped up once we got there. Carissa and I get out of the car and AJ, and Kiani stayed behind.

Kiani is not one for altercations, so that was best, and AJ has kicked the hell back do you hear me? I didn't even know how we were going to get him to scoot over when we came back.

We follow Makenzie through the apartment complex. Carissa asking a million questions as we walk. I'm not saying a word; I'm over here just praying that we don't go to jail tonight. I told Makenzie I didn't like Parker the day she approached us on campus. Now, look.

We finally make it the door. Makenzie's brown eyes open as big as day looks at us and whispers.

"Okay, this is the apartment right here."

"Somebody knock!" Carissa says nervously. Fuck it; I'm already here. So, I knock on the door. I look over a Makenzie who looks like she is in a daze. Whatever she's in, she better get in formation because we are already at the door.

I honestly couldn't tell you who opened the door. We walked in, and we heard the commotion of the party and the smoke from the weed in the air, but we wouldn't see a damn person insight. Here, we are looking like the three blind mice hands on the wall feeling for a light switch.

Things happened to perfectly because, in an instant, a flicker of light came on at the end of the room where Parker and her friends were sitting. Parker and Kenz make eye contact. Parker stands up with her short small frame and gigantic breast, looking like they will cause her to fall forward, puts hands on her hip like she was ready to argue. Poor girl, she didn't know who she been fucking with.

It was like a bull was let out of its cage. Makenzie was on the go! In a flash, she charged over to Parker.

BOP BOP BOOM!

Makenzie punches the girl until she fell back into the couch.

Carissa and I run behind to ensure none of these chicks try to jump in.

"All hell, Nah! Wtf is going on aye break it up."

A tall white boy with a voice of black guy from New York somewhere grabs Kenz by her waist out of all the commotion.

"Yo what the fuck you doing ma!" he asked shaking her by her arms

"Come on Kenz let's go; we gotta go!" I yell as I yank her out of his grip.

Carissa, Makenzie and I dashed out of the apartment. Trying not to make ourselves seem so obvious we started to walk once we got far enough from the door. We saw the security, waved past him, and made it to the car outside of the apartment.

"What happened did y'all do it," AJ asks

"Hell yeah! I got that bitch; she thought we were still about to talk when I told her no more talking period!" Makenzie was so pumped up; she wanted to tag that ass for a minute since their twitter altercation last semester.

"Girl, somebody in there is messy as hell!" I say as I push AJ over to make room in the car.

"I know, right?!" Says Carissa

"Like who opened the door for us and who turned on that light by the couch she was at?" Makenzie says as she reapplies her lip-gloss in the sun visor mirror.

"I don't know, but we need to get the hell out of dodge before somebody calls the police or something," Kiani says, clearly she was ready to go.

We drop AJ off to the off-campus dorms. Ride down Bellflower Blvd bumping some RJ until we got to Mc Donald's to get a late-night meal. Once we arrived back to the main campus dorms, we ate, took our showers and gossiped about the night and got ready for bed. Suddenly, Makenzie receives a call on her phone.

Bzzzzzzzzzz Bzzzzzzzzzzzzzzz

"Girl! It's Parker calling my phone y'all!"

Kenz puts the phone on speaker.

"Hello?"

There was a lot of yelling and commotion going on, on the other end of the phone. And finally, someone makes their presence on the phone.

"Um... hello this is Parker's mentor, and I believe what you did tonight was some bull shit, you didn't give her a warning or anything. Why don't you guys pull up to the park right now and give her a fair one?"

At that point, I was through with them! We had dropped AJ off, took showers and everything and there just now calling? Get the hell out of here!

More commotion comes from the background.

"Fuck that put me on the phone," you could hear another girl say in the background.

"Hello!" the chick yells into the phone furious.

"Um... in the midst of you hitting Parker, you punched me in my fucking face, Makenzie! That wasn't cool!"

"Oh, well! You shouldn't have been in my fucking way!" Makenzie says with a roll of her neck.

"Pull up to the park and give Parker a fair one right now!" Another chick from the other side of the phone yells.

"Girl bye it's almost two hours later and y'all just now calling, y'all bitches weak as fuck!" Makenzie going back and forth with them but I'm exhausted with the whole situation.

"Kenz, get off the phone with them, they are bull shit," I say in a stern voice, this shit was going nowhere fast.

Makenzie hangs up. They called a couple more times, but we were over it and ready to go to sleep.

"Ugh.... my finger is throbbing I just got this full set the other day," Makenzie says, rubbing her right hand and looking at her hot pink stiletto set in disgust.

"Well, girl we are gonna have to hit the nail shop tomorrow or something," Kiani says tying up her hair before she found her space on this XL twin bed. Don't ask me how all of us fit on that little ass bed. But we made it work, and it was always quite comfortable.

Makenzie sat up at her desk talking to that damn Jeremy updating him on what happened. As you can tell, I'm not a fan of his, but if she likes it, I love it.

"Alright y'all, I'm about to sleep in Jeremy's dorm... I'll see y'all in the morning" Makenzie says as she grabs her bag

"Good more legroom for me" Carissa jokes.

You would think we stayed up talking about what transpired but chile we were beaten. So, we went off to sleep. Some night we had.

Now off I go to pick up Judith from work at the hospital. I had to beg her practically to get a job y'all. She, not the type to take care of business. So to make this working woman shit as simple as possible for her, I've made it my duty to pick her up and drop her off.

On my way to the hospital I give Judith a call, I haven't been home in a couple of days hanging out with my girls, and I just wanted to chat.

"Hey babe, I'm almost to the hospital now you wouldn't believe the night we had!"

"Oh for real? Quick in response, like she was trying to get off the phone.

"Aye bae look, you ain't gotta pick me up though, I got a ride from my coworker" This bitch lost her mind.

"Who the hell is your coworker?" I questioned, I can barely get her to stay stable at a job let alone make friends.

"Man..... don't start that shit Miranda," She said like I was getting on her nerves.

People will try to make you feel like you're crazy when they are doing shit they have no business doing. But this bitch doesn't have mind control over me, and I ain't the one nor the two.

I hung up on her ass and pressed my feet on that gas to get to the City Beach Hospital to see what coworker she think of taking her home. Y'all may think I'm jumping the gun, but Judith, she always comes out the woodworks with these "friends" if you know what I mean. If you don't know, let me make it simple for you. The bitch is a cheater!

I arrive at the hospital and drive into the employee parking lot to see Judith walking hand in hand out the hospital with a brown skin curly head girl in scrubs. I spotted them heading towards a black BMW with the license plate TAYLOOR.

I give her phone another ring while watching her see if she would answer. That old Young Ma knock off looking bitch ignored my call!

"Now, she was not answering her phone, and she knew I was on my way!" I say out loud to myself angrily.

"Talking about she had a ride, yeah bitch I'm your ride," I say to myself as I send her some angry text telling her to answer the phone.

I park my car some distance away and watch and see what she do with this girl. What I did see didn't make me feel any better about the situation. Judith is being so careful with this chick. She opened the door for her while helping her into the passenger side of the car. She goes all out, putting on the damn girl's seat belt or shoot, did she lean in for a kiss?

Then she has the nerve to be walking around to the driver's side and getting in like she about to drive her and the girl home.

"That's it; I'm getting out of the car. Who is this chick?"
I give myself a pep talk as I walk toward the car, ready
for whatever. I think Makenzie is wearing off on me.

Chapter 4
Kiani Storm

"Damn Stormy you look damn good," I tell myself standing in front of my closet mirror in my bedroom.

I had on a House of CB nude over the shoulder bandage dress that looked amazing over my deep bronze skin and some gold studded Louboutin pumps. I wore my hair in a slick, dramatically long ponytail and wore natural makeup with a dark lined nude lip. I just knew I was that girl tonight.

Tonight was the night I was finally going to go all the way with Carter, Cavi if the streets are asking. We have only been dating about nine months now, but ya girl is in love. He bought me this outfit for our date tonight, but I have no clue where we're going. Leave it up to me, and

I would have been fine staying in the house watching movies. But it was my twentieth birthday, and Carter said he wanted to show me something special.

Carter was only twenty-two, but he had the wisdom of someone much older. He was always putting me up on the game of the streets. Making sure I don't get caught up in the fast life of the streets and stay classy and ladylike. He never had me drive into no spots or go into the hood with him. Carter did not play that shit any.

He and Makenzie's birthday is around the same time. When he saw her at her last party, he gave her two-hundred dollars. She was sold and liked him ever since. My friends went to school in Long Beach, but Carter and I lived in the Valley, I went to Northridge and majored in marketing.

I know you're wondering how did things with him and I moved so fast. How are we living together but we haven't even had sex yet? Well, from the day the first date we met after talking on Instagram for three months prior, we were inseparable. And hey, I'm dealing with a hood nigga with money okay. I can't be giving it up the goods so quickly. Surprisingly he hasn't pressed me about sex either. It's low key nerve-racking wondering why he hasn't made a move yet either. It makes me want to jump his guns even more.

"Aye cuh, I gotta go."

"Nigga I got plans with my girl tonight."

"Did that little nigga Jbone pick up my package?"

"Alright bet, have him drop it off at the spot tonight, you know what to do after that." He hangs up the phone pulls out a backwood and glances up at me with excitement.

"Aye baby you ready to go? You are always taking forever, girl!" He comes up behind me and wraps his arms around my waist. I inhale deeply to get a good whiff of the YSL sport cologne he was wearing. Damn, he smells good.

"Yeah I'm ready, are you done talking on the damn phone?"

" Don't start that shit up cuh, I gotta making these phone calls to keep yo fine ass in Gucci and gold," He says playfully followed by a big smack on my ass

Whack!

After taking our couple goals pictures for the gram, we head to my mystery birthday celebration location. We arrive at the Westin Bonaventura Hotel. We had to go up the Elevator, go to the 35th floor, and the waiter of LA Prime greeted us. I can get used to this I think to myself, as the waiter directed us to our table.

When we got to our table, there were already six dozens of roses surrounding our table which was lit by beautiful candlelight. Tears ran down my face, uncontrollably. Carter then pulled my chair out for me to sit. He looked damn good tonight. Caramel skin hottie with four slick braids going straight back, he got that easily managed hair if you know what I mean — wearing a red and black Kenzo sweater with some black destroyed Dsquared2 jeans and some black Dolce and Gabbana sneakers. He had on a diamond-studded Rolex and a chain with 100 years emblem to match mine. One hundred years is something we would say to each other every time we get off the phone because that's how long we plan on making our relationship last. My baby was hot boy certified.

The view was impeccable, high rise buildings everywhere, looking down to see a sky view of the city was all needed. Sharing this space with him made me feel like the city was ours.

"I ain't never loved any girl as I love you, Stormy." Tears began to run down my face all over again, and I know my makeup was through at this point.

"Your everything a nigga always wanted in his girl, you got yo shit together, you smart, beautiful and a true ride or die" I reach out and hold his hand across the table.

"I know you in school and shit, and you are not trying to plan anything of the rip.... but I was wondering, would you stop playing and make this shit official with a nigga?" Is he serious? I thought to myself. I sat there, hands to my mouth in total shock for a minute. It was like the whole room had stopped.

"Man cuh, on the set I know you heard me Kiani." Oh shit, he's using my first name, I better say something before he gets to acting crazy in here.

"Of course, I'll marry you, Carter, I love you so much, baby." He smiles. He pulls out a black box out of his pocket and opens it up. The ring was breathtaking, a 3-carat diamond halo ring with diamonds dancing around the whole gold band. He placed the ring on my finger, looked into my eyes and told me, " You officially Lady Cavi now Storm."

༄

We make it to the house, and I'm ready, okay! It's no way we were going to go to bed another night without getting busy. I rush to the bathroom to shower, and there is a big fluffy white robe with a lighting bolt embellished in Swarovski crystals on the back with slippers to match. He got me a robe with my makeup logo put on the back, he is for sure going to get it tonight.

I shower and walk into the bedroom, wrapped in my new robe and nothing underneath. I don't see him in the bedroom, and I quickly head to the living room where I find him sitting on the couch watching ESPN drinking out of a red cup. I head toward the from of the T.V. and turn it off.

"Watch out with that shit Kiani I was watching the game, and I got money on that shit."

I ignore him, face his direction, and drop my robe to the ground. He re-adjusts himself on the couch with a slight grin.

"Bring yo ass over here, man." I walked towards the couch, fully exposed. As soon as I get within arms reach, he grabs me up by my waist kissing my lower lips passionately.

He places me on the couch carefully like he didn't want to hurt any part of my body, and then places my legs on his shoulders. He was licking and sucking my pussy to pure ecstasy. I arched my back and let out a loud moan. I try to escape his grip of my thighs, but there is no escape of what he has in store for my body tonight.

With one hand, he takes his fingers and presses them into my dripping walls while massaging my clit with his thumb. With his other hand, he pulls down his pants, exposing his blue Calvin Klein boxer briefs with his throbbing man parts. He pulls his fingers out of my soaking walls and licks them free of my juices. My mouth drops.

I'm ready he can stop playing with me, I think to myself as I caress my nipples sensually playing with my gold heart piercings. He pulls out his full parts that stood at attention, ready for me. He leans down, kisses me gently on my lips and pushes himself into my throbbing walls.

Wait.. why don't I feel nothing?

"What the fuck cuh... my shit tripping."

He then sits up and aggressively strokes himself, getting hard but not staying hard long enough.

" Man cuh .. come here baby give me some head real quick." This is not what I had in mind for the first time.

As I get ready to get low, I notice a bottle of lean and a sprite bottle sitting on the floor. This nigga is high, that's why he can stay up — shaking my damn head. This is going to be a long fucking night.

Chapter 5
Carissa Humphrey

"Mama! Ma! .... is anybody here?"

"Mama not here man shut up people sleep!" My annoying big brother Cassidy screamed from the back room.

"Well excuse the fuck outta me damn," I just made it in the house from pulling a double at work, and I was tired as hell. On the days I don't have class, I been working overtime to make sure Niko has some money on his books.

Niko was my boyfriend of on and off five years, and I don't know anything but him, he is my first true love. He has been fighting this case for about three months now, and every time we go to court, the stupid ass

DA keeps requesting more time. We go back to court tomorrow, and I can't do anything but pray they let my baby home.

I don't know what was going to happen with his case. I have just been doing my part right now making sure he straight because that's what good girlfriends do.

"Since you have done woke a nigga up, you got a letter from that little nigga Niko today"

"Forreal ?! Where is it?" I dashed to the counter where my mom kept the mail and began sorting through.

" I wish you leave that nigga alone, he ain't no good. You a sweet girl, you don't have no business dating some nigga in jail."

I cut my eye at him in annoyance. Who is he to judge Niko? All the stress he has put momma and me through going in and out of jail during his high school years. My momma almost lost the house trying to get him a lawyer one time.

"Look I don't wanna hear that Cassidy, nobody was telling Nunu that when she was waiting for you to come home."

"Yeah because I'm that N I G G A," he says playfully.

"Plus, this foo doesn't do anything for you. Look at you working yourself half to death to make sure he eats. That's out."

I mean he had a point, I do hold a lot of the weight in Niko's and my relationship. But he has just been dealt a tough hand, and he was getting better. He had just got a Twic card to work at the oil refinery, and we had just started to look for apartments.

"Cassidy leave me alone, and I just got off work. I'm tired, and I want to read my letter alright."

"Man whatever, you heard what I said! If little homie hurt you, that's his head."

I walk upstairs to my room, take a long relaxing shower and cuddle up with my letter as if it was Niko himself. Big day ahead of me tomorrow, we go to court, I hope they let him come home this time.

∽

The courtroom is packed with people waiting to see which Division their case is going to be sent to. I arrived at the courtroom just in enough time to hear his name.

"Niko Grant will be in Division 20 today."

I stand outside to speak with his lawyer. Between his books and this damn lawyer fee, I was going to work my self to death.

" Hey, Carissa how is it going?" His layer, Lauren says.

"I'm alright," I say in a defeated voice.

"Do you have any updates on his case, do you think they will let him come home today ?" Twiddling my thumbs nervously. I'm trying to be hopeful because I don't know how much more of this jail shit a girl can take.

"Well you know since this is his first offense, I think I may be able to get the judge to count the time he has been in already as timed served if he pleaded guilty."

Pleaded guilty? It's always a catch with these freaking layers I swear. What am I busting my ass paying her for?

"Well have you talked to Niko about pleading guilty?" She asks me. I stare down at my hands, unsure. "I don't think he is going to want to do that."

"Well with this possession with the intent to distribute charges and this gun charge that maybe his only option."

I mean I guess she had a point. How the hell do you prove intent? Before I was able to finish our conversation, I had to excuse my self and dash to the restroom.

Here I am in this court bathroom stall hunched over throwing up. I've missed my period that lasts two months, but I figure it was maybe just the stress of work, school, and Niko going to jail.

"Lord, I don't have time for this shit," I say to the man up above as clean myself up and head upstairs to Division 20 to this hearing. I don't know what was to come of this case, or if I was pregnant. But I need Niko's ass to take this freaking deal or whatever he has to do and come home.

Chapter 6
Makenzie Gray

It's been a couple of months since the fight between Parker and me, and boy I tell ya, word travels fast around these LBC parts. Jeremy and I have been closer than ever, spending the night with each other every night. We even spent Easter with his family, and he met my mom and grandma. Recently we had a little pregnancy scare, but he and I both decided now wasn't the time to have kids because we were still in school and working on ourselves. I'd be lying if I said it was something I want to do. I tried to keep my baby, but Jeremy made it very clear it was not something he would be in support of and who wants to force a nigga to be ready, you know? Since then he has been very supportive emotionally, ya girl has been going through it. It seems as he was the devil while I was pregnant saying anything to get me to get rid of our baby. Now that its all said and done, he has been a damn angel kissing my ass. This situation has made me lose respect for him in so many ways and my self. I find myself crying at the sight of a dude loving his girl and their baby, wishing I had a nigga that wanted me to carry his seed. I don't know if I could forgive myself for this shit. But I know that after such a sacrifice for this relationship and what we were going through, nothing could break us. I have given everything to make this work.

"Good morning Jeremy "

"Morning Kenz, what you got planned for today, baby?"

"Just class and then I think I may hit an informational for a club on campus."

"That sounds cool, I have to do some homework tonight, and then I gotta get prepared for a test I got next week." He says while brushing his hair and packing his backpack with textbooks and notepads.

Jeremy was so fine to me. Chocolate skin with a smile that would light up a room. As much as he brushed that damn hair, you already know them waves were on swim-swim. He wasn't the tallest nigga, average in height, but his charm and confidence kept me drawn.

I sit up in his bed and look at his notifications on his phone. I see Parker's name with a smiley and heart emoji next to it with the text saying

PARKER: Can't wait to see you tonight.

I play it cool because I didn't want him to know I was looking through his stuff.

"Well, link up tonight? We can study together."

"Naw, not tonight baby I gotta study, you know I can't keep my focus when you here."

"Yeah, Yeah whatever Mac. I'll see you later then."

"Come here Kenz, I hate when you get pouty," he says, grabbing my arm and wrapping his arms around my shoulders.

"I'm not pouty, and you just got a lot of excuses."

With an exasperated expression, he threw his arms up in defeat.

"Makenzie, you know what I ain't got time for this, I told you I would see you later, alright?"

"Oh, so you wanna pick a fucking fight? Have you been hanging with me and studying now all of a sudden you can't? What's the issue, Mac? What changed?!"

"I want some fucking space, alright! Damn, you wanna hang out every day"

He thinks I was fucking stupid. I saw him put that phone on silent last night before we went to sleep. This guy has even gone the extreme to get a tinted screen protector so I can't see who he is talking to.

"You don't think I know what you are doing tonight, Mac?!"

Tears, rolling down my eyes from hurt and humiliation.

"I just got in a fight with this girl, she and her friends don't like me and tried to hit me with a freaking car! And it was all over you! I just let go of a baby! for you!"

I just felt so stupid. I was fighting so hard for his love. What was it about him that made me feel like he was worth it. I think it was maybe the thrill of it all. Wanting to be with the guy that I believed everyone fawned over.

Maybe the feeling of fighting for a man's love was all too familiar for me. My daddy always had a new girlfriend or baby momma trying to compete with me. "Why you giving her all that money Drew" his wife would say. "I hope when I have my daughter, she doesn't come out dark-skinned like you, I don't want no dark ass baby" some shit she would say every time dad would leave the room during her pregnancy.

It was just last month over Christmas break when my dad and I got in the biggest fight we've ever had.

My dad had just taken me to the car dealership to purchase and car and then changed his mind at the desk when they started to do paperwork. My dad has the habit of having me at the register with items and changing his mind when it's time to commit and pay. It was so embarrassing. Soon after him changing his mind about buying my car, he went and bought his wife, his mom, and himself a brand new car from the dealership.

My mom is was not feeling me continually being disappointed, so she went to the dealership and bought me my blueberry Honda Civic coupe. I was so excited, and Christmas was right around the corner. Thus, being that my mom bought my car, I ask my daddy for 40 dollars to purchase her a gift. He didn't reply and screened my calls for the entire week. I was livid, and I sent him a text letting him know how I felt.

ME: You know what daddy every time I need you for something, you always let me down. I'm over being let down by you.

Bzzzzzzz

DADDY: Well quite frankly, your 18 years old now and I have two other daughters, I don't need you as a daughter anymore you dead to me.

ME: Fuck You then my nigga!

DADDY: Fuck you to hoe.

I ran to my grandpa's room crying and told him what my dad had said to me. He wasn't one for emotional support. He just said.

"He ain't never been any daddy to you anyway, and I'm yo daddy."

Although my grandfather stood in and took that father role, it broke my heart, knowing my dad was out in this world with a new family, loving his other kids and not me, his firstborn.

I believe that it was from that day; I never wanted to lose a man I loved to no other female. And I didn't want to lose to no female, especially weak ass Parker. Why couldn't I get him to be a one-woman man to just me?

"Makenzie…" he says in a proper mild manner tone.

"Your problems with people are not mine, and I don't have a problem with Parker; she didn't do anything to me… I haven't been speaking to her because of you, and I feel like that isn't fair to me. And I don't need a baby right now I have too much going on"

This nigga must have lost his damn mind. I'm so over this bull shit with him. It was becoming to be exhausting. I sacrificed everything for this to work.

"What do you mean, why did you get my nails fixed and spend so much time with me after that fight then?" I ask him, eyes bloodshot red and tears rolling down my face.

"Because I care for you, but I have the right to care for other people too, your not being fair to me Kenz."

Well shit maybe he has a point we weren't 'official' yet, but we have been doing all the couple things and emotionally. And shit, after everything we were going through the nerve of this nigga to pull an official label out there to me. I can't take it.

I left Jeremy's room furious, tears rolling down my eyes. I went to my dorm to dress. But my nosey nature couldn't help but to check twitter and see what Jeremy or Parker has posted on their page.

JMAC: Nipsey new shit is the vibe all year!

JMAC: @miniP where the weed at?

JMAC: @PrincessTay playing with me, man, where are you, princess?

Wait who the fuck is PrincessTay? I'm over here pressed about Parker, and he only hit her up to smoke. It seems like I have a whole other chick to worry about.

I click on her page and look at her bio and is see a ring emoji with a @JMAC next to it and a newly uploaded picture of an ultrasound.

Chapter 7
Carissa Humphrey

"I've been craving this cinnamon roll all day! I wish they hurry up with my shit," Makenzie's greedy self says as she looks looking around at everyone's tables around us who have already been served in Polly's Pies.

Miranda, Makenzie, and I had skipped our afternoon African Dance class for some mid-day brunch.

"So, what's tea sistahs?" Miranda asked bob, bouncing and waving in the air while sipping her orange juice.

"Girllll, we went to court last week, and they presented Niko with a deal." Just speaking it out loud to anyone gets my stomach to turn.

"Well, that's good. What's the deal?"

"The deal is two years, and he gets some time knocked off for the time he is doing right now, but I don't have time for that I need him home like today" I've been sicker than ever lately and haven't been able to work my full shifts at work. Miranda saw the sadness in my eyes, and I guess she decided to switch the subject.

"Chileeeee, y'all wouldn't believe what happened when I was picking up Judith from work."

"Girl, I'm on my way to pick her up, and she tells me she has a ride already and not to pick her up, what kinda inconsiderate shit is that!"

Judith did have a fascinating history of making 'friends,' but lately, she been kissing the ground Miranda walks on. Honestly, it could all be in Miranda's head, once a person betrays your trust once you always think something is up.

Miranda continued to explain. " I could understand if she called well before she knew I was on my way, but damn JuJu how inconsiderate To my time can you be!"

Makenzie, wanting to get to the juicy part, stared blankly at Miranda and said, "Well, what happened?"

"When I pulled up, I saw her holding some coworkers hand walking her to her car, and getting in the driver seat." Couldn't be me, I'm so happy Niko didn't have me around here looking stupid with females. Shoot I'm already looking crazy and every other aspect of our relationship.

Miranda continued the story. " Girl I must have hopped out of that car so quick, knocked on that drive window like 'what the hell is up Judith.'"

Makenzie sips on her water all into the drama. " So what did her Muthafuckin ass say, girl?"

So she gets out of the car and immediately is trying to calm me down talking about "It's not what it looks like Miranda! I gotta take her home cause she pregnant and fell out at work today!"

I don't know if I could fall for that bull. I gave Miranda the bishhhh please look immediately.

"When I was looking at that passenger seat, the girl was pregnant, she had a little belly, and she was throwing up in a hospital bag."

Kenz starts cracking up, " Haha I bet yo ass felt bad acting a fool at that job."

" Girl, hell naw because she should have explained that on the phone, but I followed her to the girl house anyway and gave the girl some of my ginger candy's in my purse and me and Judith went home."

"Now she got the nerve to have me in the dog house for embarrassing her at work in front of her co-workers."

"That's what yo ass get for trying to pull at me!" Makenzie jokes.

"Girl bye I'm a thug too!" Miranda says in her valley girl tone.

"Speaking of a thug, this thug feels dumb as hell, I went on Twitter and saw that Jeremy got some girl pregnant girl."

Just even speaking it out loud, visibly broke Makenzie's heart. If you were at school, you didn't see him without her or her without him. I know my friend loves that damn boy, but I can't stand him. I mean every nigga has his flaws, but this was one arrogant bastard.

"Oh, wow! Well, what did you say to him, Kenz?"

She sips her drink and fiddles with her hands nervously. "I ... I didn't say anything yet. Honestly, I'm waiting for him to break the news to me himself."

"Girl, are you going to keep dealing with him ?" At this point, Miranda was fed up with Jeremy and his antics.

"Well, I don't know for sure if it's his or what the facts, y'all I'm in denial I don't get when he has the time we are together 24/7!"

Tears roll down my girl's face, and I just felt so bad for her because he plays on her emotions. It's crazy because when you see them together, he is so in love with her, but the things she says he does when nobody is around is freaking crazy.

Our food finally arrived, and what I was once craving, I can't even bear the smell of. To satisfy my hunger, I tried to cut a piece of the cinnamon roll to eat, but it was so nasty. I cannot bear the sight or smell of some greasy food, and this buttered cinnamon bun and sausage wasn't cutting it. I excused myself from the table as calmly as I could and walked swiftly to the bathroom.

Here I am again in another freaking public place, hunched over throwing up. It seemed like it was getting worse as the weeks go by, and I didn't want to face the reality of what may be happening in my body knowing I may have to do it by myself.

I just began to cry uncontrollably in the bathroom stall alone. , suddenly there was a knock on my stall.

"Carissa?! Is that you in here? What's going on pooh?" Makenzie yells whirl peeping through the door, making eye contact with me.

"I don't feel too good, is it okay if we leave when get done in the bathroom?" I reply, trying to contain my tears.

"Girl, we already paid for that food and packed up, whenever you come out of that stall, we taking you home," Miranda says by the stall door. Damn, I love these bitches.

I haven't told them about the possibility of me being pregnant yet or how stressed I been about Niko's case. But that didn't matter; they didn't need to know the details. They just knew that I wasn't okay, and they are right here. This is what friendship is all about.

I come out of the bathroom stall, clean myself up start heading out of the restaurant. There I am welcomed by Makenzie and Miranda. We get in Makenzie's blue Honda Civic, blast our favorite Anticipation mixtape by Trey Songz and head back to Makenzie's dorm.

Suddenly Makenzie turns the music down and the car, and there is an awkward silence.

"Are you pregnant hoe?" Kenz gets on my fucking nerves. I couldn't do anything but laugh.

"I don't know for sure I haven't taken any test" looking down at my fingers together in a nervous manner.

Miranda, who was sitting in the front passenger seat points at a Target and says, "Kenz pull over to this store we about to find out today."

⚉

We make it to the Lakeview dorm parking lot and head towards Makenzie's dorm. As we were walking to the K building, we see Jeremy and Parker walking towards the parking lot.

Makenzie stood stagnant, and her eyes were as a buck like a bull ready to charge. Miranda and I look at each other fearing what Makenzie was going to do next. But to our surprise Makenzie didn't say a word, she walked straight past them. Not before giving Jeremy and Parker a deadly look.

Jeremy looked back with a smile. I don't care what anyone says, and he was one messy nigga. He enjoyed making Makenzie mad with other girls when they were not speaking.

We make it to Makenzie's dorm room, and as she plops on her bed, she immediately says, " go take the test hoochie." Oh lawddd, I wasn't ready to take a test, it's already too much going on. Miranda takes the test out of the pharmacy back and throws it on the bed.

"Go ahead girl, because if TT baby in there you need to know so you can have your check-ups and daily vitamins."

Miranda has lost her damn mind, 'TT baby?' What am I'm about to do with a baby with my man up under the damn jailhouse? I rolled my eyes in annoyance and headed towards the suite bathroom.

"How the hell do you even use this thing ?" I mumble to myself as I close the stall door.

I read the back of the package it says to pee on it for 10 seconds or to pee in a cup and place the stick in the cup. I don't have a cup, but I for damn sure don't think I can pee that long. You know what, forget it let's get it over with.

I take the pregnancy test out and open the top covering. I drank plenty of water all day, so I knew I had to go. I pop a squat hovering over the toilet while holding the stick underneath.

Damn, pee didn't act right, spraying everywhere all over the toilet seat. Hopefully, enough landed on this stick because this is annoying as fuck.

I clean and flush the toilet, wrap the test in tissue paper, and head to the sink to wash my hands. While washing my hands, I give myself a big pep talk. "Alright Rissa, no matter what this shit says you got it, girl, you got the hustle for it."

The directions say to set it on a flat surface for three minutes, so I grab some more paper towels and walk into Kenz room, sitting it right on her desk.

"Ughhhhh... why you sit that shit on my desk like that?"

I chuckled, "I put some paper towels down, and oh well, hoe! You wanted me to take a test so bad, so here it goes!" I say casually and plop on her bed as I lived there.

"How long do we have to wait?" Miranda asks.

"It says three minutes, it for sure already been one so we just have to wait and see."

Makenzie hovers over the test every two seconds to see if two lines appear. "I think the second one is coming in right now!"

"Girl stop looking, I don't want to look until all the time on the directions has passed."

I was nervous as hell I can't even front, I wish I was doing this with Niko instead and not with my girls. Don't get me wrong I love them, but I never wanted this life for myself pregnant in college with my nigga in jail. I always gave a side-eye to bitches like this, now look at me.

So much was going through my mind while we sit awkwardly in Makenzie's room waiting for my test results. My phone rings.

"Rissa, Niko calling."

I'm freaking stuck, and I can't even move. I just picked up this stick, and it has two lines.

"Rissa! He calling you" Miranda says again.

" Girl I can't fucking talk to him right now, I don't even know how imma tell him this shit," test in hand looking down at two strong lines.

"Tell him what? ... Ohh shit you picked up the test, you pregnant ?" Makenzie throws her laptop to the side and hops from her bed to look over my should at the test.

"Aww friend you about to be a mommy... are you okay though?

The water show began. I start crying. Kenz gave me the biggest bear hug while I sob in her arms. Miranda got up to join wiping my tears and placing a kiss on my cheek. My friends were everything I needed at this moment.

My phone rings again.

What a way to kill the moment. I look over at my phone, and it's Niko's bald ass mom who cannot stand me. I inhale deeply as I answer the phone.

"Sniff... Hey Ms.Kiesha, how are you doing?"

"Uh-huh, I'm alright. Niko said you were not answering the phone; wanted me to call, and tell you to pick up." This bitch was so rude she doesn't like me. I have been nothing but good to her son. I'm the only person who never misses a court date, but she still acts like I'm the girlfriend that ain't about shit.

"I'm on campus right now I wasn't by my phone, but I'll catch the next call." Loud music in her background. It always seemed like it was a party going on at her house.

"Hey momma I'm coming over to do Nakea's hair." I heard a familiar voice in the background.

It sounds like Niko's big sister homegirl that he used to mess around with during one of our long breakups. His momma loved that broad she always was coming around the house trying to be in Niko's face when we got back together, he dismissed that shit quick, but his messy ass mom won't let her go.

"Is that Faith?"

"Yeah, she is about to do Nakea hair for their visit to see Niko tomorrow." What the hell does she mean their visit?

"Is that Faith?"

"Yeah, she is about to do Nakea hair for their visit to see Niko tomorrow." What the hell does she mean their visit?

"Wait a min Faith going too?"

"How else is Nakea going to go she doesn't have no car right now remember her accident?" That's out, she trying to play me. But out of respect for his mom I just politely said. "Ok well, I'll answer the next call. I have to go."

Click

This is too much, why is she taking Faith with her to see Niko? Fuck, that whole family when I have my baby I'm not bringing him or her around until Niko comes home. Ms.Kiesha liked project bitches, charity case girls who didn't have shit going but looking fly for the hood. She didn't understand me, I had my parents and my stability, im in college and doing my own thing. I think she may be jealous of a young boss bish like me.

I don't mean to toot my own horn, but I am a bad one. I was your definition of slim thick. Tiny brown skin chick with some ass on her with a baby doll face. Light brown eyes with long wispy lashes that looked like I got a volume set from the esthetician. Thick long brown hair that I kept in a silk press with perfectly trimmed ends.

I was admitted into the nursing program after my first year of undergrad because I had already gotten my associate's degree in high school, and I been on a steady grind. Ms.Keisha wanted her son to have a girlfriend that worshiped her, and she ain't have shit for me to look up to. She lived off social security and county checks but was fully able to work, she was just a fly bum and had all the clout in the hood for rocking the hottest fashions.

Ghetto bitches always had all the designers. I didn't get it. All that didn't matter to me though I am a modest dresser, not to focus on fashion more focused on making my money and stacking. I have been doing nails on campus and at home as a side job to make some extra money. I been becoming pretty popular for it, recently I just had a top Instagram model Trix Kasey do a promotional shoot for my winter acrylic sale.

Faith was a cute girl, but she wasn't me, and Niko knew it. That's why he got his ass together and came home. She claims to have been pregnant by him in those couple months we broke up and they were together, but she miscarried. Now every year she writing some long posts on social media talking about "Knick Grant, her son in the sky." She wasn't even far enough along to know what she was having anyway.

Yeah, Niko and I have had our trouble, but he knows where home is, and he knows who wifey is period.

"Girl, what Ms.Keisha messy ass want today?" Makenzie asked, laying in my lap watching the new episode of The Side Chicks of Hip Hop.

"Girl she doesn't want shit, it sounds like she just wanted me to know that Faith was going to see Niko with Nakea."

Miranda was curled up on the second bed fast asleep, and I guess she was tired from that Cinnamon Roll. So Kenz and I used this time to catch up further since I darted to the restroom at our lunch date.

"Girl she is out of it!" Makenzie is so dramatic, but she doesn't play about me that's my sister for real.

"I'm not even tripping because Niko gone cuss Nakea out for bringing Faith anyway, it ain't like he far he only downtown right now she can Uber. He's going to know she is being messy."

I had a lot of faith, no pun intended in Niko. He did his shit when we broke up, and we got through that, but he lets nobody cross me. So, I don't have time to stress over no damn Faith or his messy ass family.

My phone rings again, and it lights up as Niko with a lock and red heart. Yeah, I became one of those girls that save the jail number. I answer it immediately and listen to this Global Tel Link operator tell me how many minutes I got left. I always make sure its money on the phone, so I wasn't even listening to her ass. Like damn, tell me to press five already! After what seems like forever I press five and hear a slam — followed by hearing the most amazing sound, the love of my life.

"Aye baby what's wrong? You haven't been answering a nigga's calls all day ... I got some good news too!"

See the difference between my nigga and everybody else's is that their man would be calling pressing being mad and mean and shit for not answering the phone. But not my baby he knew something had to be wrong. Now that I know I'm pregnant, I was nervous as ever to hear the news.

"I talked to my lawyer today; she told me it's a good chance I could come home next court date." He says in a gleeful tone.

"Wait really; she told me to talk to you about taking the deal cause she wasn't sure how it would turn out with the evidence."

I hear a big huff on his end, I could tell he was getting irritated with the thought of taking a deal.

"Aye blood, I ain't taking no Muthafuckin deal with no time! I don't even know why she told you that bull shit man."

"Well, what happened, so different papa why she saying you gone come home?" I'm so confused. His story and what the Lawyer said the last court date two different things.

"Aye baby, don't trip just know I'm coming home, and my lawyer talked to her about giving me probation and community service instead of that bull shit she was telling you."

What a relief, if that's what they are planning to do. I'm more excited to tell him this news. I wave bye to Makenzie and kiss Miranda's sleepy self on the cheek, leave the dorm and head towards my car. I didn't want anyone to be around while I tell Niko this big news.

"Well, Niko, I have some big news to tell you myself." I'm so nervous as if he was right here in my face.

"You got some big news to tell me, huh... what's going on baby you pregnant?"

What the fuck, how did he know? I swear this boy is psychic; he always knows what I'm about to say or when something is going on with me.

"What a way to kill my surprise NIKO! How the hell did you know?" I said in an irritated tone. He needs to get out and become the male Ms.Cleo.

"Wait, you pregnant for real? Stop playing baby you gone have me too happy in this bitch. Aye, fooo my girl having my baby!!"

He yells to someone in the background.

"Who are you telling our business to, sir?"

He chuckles and then you hear some little sniffles on the phone.

"Man I was telling the little homie right here, man I'm not home with you, and you find out you about to have my baby. I'm so sorry mama I feel like the worst nigga."

I could tell he was crying in the other line and I didn't know what to say to him to make him feel at ease about this situation he has put us in. Although I knew he wanted to be here with me. The truth of the matter was he wasn't, and this was big news to find out without him.

"Well I didn't go to the doctor yet I just took at home test our next court date is in two days, so hopefully you come home... and get you a regular job, and we can go to the doctor together and be a family."

I had to throw that get a regular job shit out there because I'm ready for something stable, Kiani got her life and nigga, Judith and Miranda got their place. I'm ready for that as well.

"Look, Carissa, I love you more than anything in this fucking world girl. I ain't ever about to put us in this situation again. I know it's been hard for you to handle all this pressure I been putting on you to hold me down. When I come home you about to kick your feet up and not worry about a damn thing. I got you I love you baby momma."

He so dreamy with his ghetto self, he couldn't wait to start calling my baby momma. But I needed to hear him say he appreciated what I been doing because it has started to feel like too much on my plate; I am exhausted.

"I love you more Niko, I can't believe we are having a baby," I exclaim while wiping the tears from my cheeks.

"Shit, I can. I hid them birth control pills remember?" This fool is crazy, and he sure did hide those pills.

"Yes, I remember fool, you trapped me!"

He bursts into laughter.

"You stuck with a nigga forever baby! Aye, I gotta go imma call you after your class tomorrow. Tell Jr, I love him. Shit, I'll be home next week anyway I'll tell him myself."

I roll my eyes, and he already got his mind stuck on having a JR.

"I'll let HER know you love her, and okay baby, please call me tomorrow. I love you forever."

"And ever, baby... I'll holla at you."

After talking to Niko on the phone, I feel even more confused about the court and the outcome of his case. At least he knows I'm pregnant now, and that's out the way, I hope this baby gets him off these streets hustling, I need him home with me.

Once I arrived home, I showered did my lab assignments and got prepared for school the next day. Once I got on the bed my mind was on what was going to happen at court in two days. One thing is for sure and two things for certain. I was not going to be able to finish school and have my baby unless Niko brought his ass home.

Chapter 8
Kiani Storm

It was Valentine's Day, and I'm excited to find out what Carter has in store for the night. Lately, I have been all wrapped up in school and working on my cosmetics line. I haven't been giving him that much attention. But tonight I had a lot of tricks up my sleeve.

I booked us a suite at the JW Marriott, I already checked in and made the arrangements for the decorations in the room. It's pretty hard to buy gifts for a nigga who already got everything, so I had to get real creative.

I have been going back and forth between the hotel and our apartment all day. I told Carter not to come home because I was busy getting ready for his surprise and I didn't want him to see anything. He sounded more excited than me on the phone when I told him to meet me at the JW Marriott room 402 at nine o'clock pm. We always go out to eat in beautiful places, so I didn't care to go out this Valentine's Day I was just interested in showing him how hard I would go for him to make him feel special tonight.

I got my lingerie laid out on the hotel bed to put on once I got out of the shower. Strawberries were cut up and prepared alongside the sour cream and brown sugar I had nicely presented on my gold and cream Z Gallerie serving plate.

I already had the hotel bringing our dinner to the room at 9:30 pm that will give me enough time to get him comfortable before dinner came. Our Saks salesman Leon had already brought me the spiked royal blue Christian Louboutin shoes I had him search high and low for to give to Carter as a gift.

♫ Ooh, I'm about to dive in, woah ♫

As Trey Songz plays in the background as I practice my routine I've been learning to perform for my man tonight. Singing the words while doing the motions in the mirror.

♫ I'm about to dive in
Baby girl, hold your breath
We about to get so wet
Swimming in your body, let me dive in
You know ain't no running 'round this pool
Going under just for you, baby you
Watch me stroke left stroke, right stroke, backstroke ♫

Damn this, routine shit wasn't as easy as I thought. Imagine how hard it was going to be when I put on these stripper heels I bought from Dolls Kill. I guess today was the day to find out. I get the shoes out of the closet and put them on. My legs feel like spaghetti trying to keep balance in these bitches. But I was determined to get this routine down and popping for my baby Hotboy Cavi.

"Siri"

"Yes Kiani"

"Replay Dive in by Trey Songz"

"Ok, now playing Dive in by Trey Songz."

Finally getting my balance in these heels, I start doing the routine that my girl DancebyJes been teaching me over the past few weeks. There was a lot of floor movement and hair swinging, I never practiced in heels so high, so I was praying I didn't break my damn neck.

With a roll of my neck and a twirl of my hips, you could not tell me a damn thing about how I was gone rock his world tonight. Since the last sexual encounter, I haven't told y'all about how my baby has laid it the hell down in the bedroom.

I can't get enough of him these days, and I was one sprung bitch. I created a love coupon book that finally came in the mail last night, and I put it in a blue striped box with a big bow. This was a crip nigga, and Valentine's Day wasn't gonna make our world red. Every decoration revolving our Valentine's Day was royal blue and gold.

The balloon and flower designers I hired to decorate the suite had strict directions on insuring that the suite looked very sexy and represented Valentine's Day while still being blue.

It was getting closer to nine o'clock and time for me to make my way to the hotel, approve of the decor, shower, and do my hair and makeup. Carter always had his unique ways of making me feel special but tonight was all about him. Even though I knew he had some tricks up his sleeve.

⌇

I walk into the hotel suite, and it was drop-dead gorgeous. Clear balloons with gold glitter and blue heart balloons hang from the wall. Blue roses spelling Carter across the window ceil that displayed the beautiful view of Downtown Los Angeles. It was just breathtaking. I pay the decorators, take a shower and have my hairstylist come up to the restroom of the suite to do my hair.

"Girl this shit is the bomb in here, you hooked this shit up. I see you trying to get down that aisle huh?" Navon lived for this type of lifestyle. I was no fool that we wouldn't be as close as we're are now if my nigga and I weren't so coined up. But that my hairstylist and my boy so he gets a pass.

"Navon I just wanted to do something special for him. I was so excited about Valentine's Day cause I just wanted him to see how much he means to me and ugh, I love that boy." A little tear call itself coming down my eye and my makeup artist wasn't having it.

Putting the Q-tip in the right corner of my eye. "Girl stop that shit okay because I don't have time to redo under the eyes were already running behind."

Damn she was right it is 8:30 and I still needed to put on my lingerie and go over my dance routine one more time.

My glam team left the room, and I put on my royal blue bedazzled teddy that tied around my waist and around my neck with my silk long robe to match. I'm running around like a chicken with my head cut off lighting the candles around the room, trying not to sweat out my leave out.

My phone is lighting up, and I dash to see who it is. It's Carter oh my goodness I'm so nervous for him to see his surprise, but I missed the damn call.

Suddenly, my phone rings again, and it's my baby.

CARTER: wassup baby, you ready for daddy to pull up?

Ugh, this boy knows just what to say to get me all flustered.

ME: Yeah daddy I'm ready for you, come on up.

Carter: Open the door I got a surprise for you.

I head to the door and look out of the peephole, and it seems to be our salesmen Leon at my door, what is he doing here again?

"Leon what do you want now? Cavi is coming any minute!"

"Girl I know he told me to come too. Surprise sissy! I hope you love it!" Behind him followed five hotel workers, each holding large Chanel boxes. Damn, I can't ruin my makeup this early crying I scream and jump into Leon's arms scolding him for not letting me in on the secret.

Today is supposed to be about him, and he still found a way to make me feel like his number one lady. The hotel workers and Leon place the gifts down and leave. Shortly after, I hear another knock at the door, and it was my hunk of a man Carter.

He looked damn good in a casual Palms Angel sweatsuit and some RAF Simmons shoes with his gold draped in every gold chain he owned and what looked like a new Cuban link bracelet.

Carter was holding a box he immediately sat on the counter when he placed his eyes on me in my royal blue teddy and the glass stripper heels.

"What you trying to do tonight get a baby put in you cuh?" He says with a chuckle and swoops me in his arms, placing a big juicy kiss on my lips.

I couldn't get his hands off of me, but I wanted him to see all the surprises I had for him first.

"Wait bae I got some more surprises for you. Sit down! I'll be right back."

"Stormy stop playing with me cuh. I'm trying to get crackin right now, and you ain't even gotta do nothing else."

He was so annoying, but I been practicing this routine for weeks and it wouldn't go in vain. He was going to get the whole show.

I go to the mini-fridge and get my serving tray with my brown sugar sour cream and cut up strawberries. I sit it on the nightstand next to the bed grab my phone and play Trey Songz Dive in through the Bluetooth speaker.

I dip the strawberry in the sour cream and then into the brown sugar and feed it to him. He doesn't know it's sour cream or he would fuck with it, but it's bomb as fuck so once he ate it he licked his lips and didn't ask any questions.

I get in his lap and start to grind to the beat of the song, I twirl my hair, spin around and land in a squatted position facing his rising parts. I give it a kiss and a grab it over his clothes, stand up and walk backward slowly to the rhythm of the song

♫ *Swimming in your body, let me dive in*
You know ain't no running 'round this pool ♫

And the worst happens my damn ankles buckled while I was trying to walk away and be sexy. I heard a little laugh on his end, but he still looked intrigued. So forget it, the show must go on. I finished my routine dropping like it was hot slowing grinding the air

♫*Going under just for you, baby you*
Watch me stroke left stroke, right stroke, backstroke♫

"Kiani, come here bae, stop playing." He says in a hot and heavy voice. I got em where I want him now.

♫ *Girl, there ain't no running 'round this pool*
Ooh, I'm about to dive in
Baby girl, hold your breath
We about to get so wet
Put me to the test girl when I dive ♫

The song ended, and my routine was over. I kicked those damn heels off my feet and hobbled over to Cavi and plopped in his lap.

"You enjoy the Stormy show baby?" I asked exasperated.

"Yeah you almost broke yo damn neck trying to give me a show, but you looked good I loved it, mama." Placing a thousand kisses on my face. He picks me up and lays me on the bed. We haven't even finished opening up each other's gifts, but I guess he didn't care about that.

He grabs my feet and begins to caress and kiss them. He continues to kiss me down my leg into my inner thigh, diving into my womanhood. My baby, he knew just what to do to get me ready.

He sat up licking his lips, his dick stood at attention when I went down and licked and sucked it damn near off the bone. I'm so happy I got him to quit that damn lean it was coming into between him giving me my issue.

We made love all night I don't even remember falling to sleep all I remember is waking up on my back between his legs as if we fell asleep after climaxing for the last time with me on top. Damn what a night.

Happy Valentines Day!

Chapter 9
Nakea Grant

"Faith come on, girl, I'm ready to go!"

Today was the day I was going to see my brother locked down. He has been down for a couple of months now, and I couldn't bear to see him in there like that. It's different when it's just the homies in the set, but when it's your blood it hurts differently.

I have just been letting his little girlfriend handle all that. She swears that she is the girlfriend of the year, like she more family to Niko than my momma and me. That's why I don't like that stupid bitch cause she thinks she better.

My brother didn't like girls like me and my momma though, and he liked those goody girls that were out the way. But when he and Carissa broke up the last time I hooked him up with my best friend Faith. Everything was going good he was always at home with us and Faith was already close to the family so everything was perfect. Faith's daddy and our daddy may they Rest In Peace were best friends growing up, and they were from the same hood Niko from. So it would have been so perfect for them to stay together and keep it in the family.

But nooo my brother wanted to be with some young girl that doesn't even want him to put on for the hood or nothing. She doesn't care about our family's respect around here.

 Ever since my brother been trying to be out the way dating ole girl, niggas have been trying their luck in the set. And that's why the streets needed him to keep these little niggas straight. That's exactly what I was going up to the visit to talk to him about.

I mean, I didn't have to take Faith with me. I didn't need her for no ride, but I wanted him to see her and maybe miss her a little bit. I mean she is the only girl that has carried his seed, he gotta have some feelings for her still, right?

"Girl I'm coming, how do I look? I want him to see me looking hella fly since he hasn't seen me in a while." Faith loved my brother, and I loved her for my brother it was just a better fit. What Niko gonna do with some college girl? She doesn't even understand his struggles and what we been through.

"Faith all I know is we need to leave now, or we are gone be late to the visit."

"Alright come on I'm ready too, let's go."

On our way to the County Jail, I get a text from my baby daddy Carter. He from a different hood but we were together on and off since 9th-grade high school. Right now we weren't together, but I mean I been around before all the money shit.

Yesterday we spent Valentine's Day together. We didn't do anything that night because my momma wasn't trying to watch Cj. So we just went to Bossa Nova, I gave him some sloppy toppy and dropped it down low at his spot in the hood, and he sent me and Faith to Spa Palace. It was lovely. He always trying to do something nice for me. I appreciate him.

I know he got a new bitch, I know all about Kiani fuck her! That's probably why I don't like Carissa even more because I know that's her best friend. Carissa never brought her friends around my family, so I doubt the girl knew that was my baby daddy but still. Hell, Carissa never even seen my baby daddy because she makes it her duty not to come to any of our family events. I told y'all she thinks she better.

BABYDADDY: Imma come to pick up Cj tomorrow night, so he can spend the week with me. How was the spa?

ME: Okay, I'll have his bag ready, I may be at work. And yes we had a blast thank you baby daddy ; -* I'm going to see Niko

BABYDADDY: That's good. I love y'all. Tell my young nigga I said to stay up and I put some money on his books yesterday.

See how caring he is, no matter what he still made sure we were a family. That's what that bitch Kiani was missing she could never be FAMILY because that's me. I got his JR I got his firstborn nobody can take that away.

We make it to the jail, and the visitation line is long as hell. Good thing we got here an hour and a half before the visit. Niko knew I was coming, but he didn't know I was coming with Faith I hope he was excited to see her.

Faith over here shellacking on her lipgloss by the pounds trying to make sure she looked good for my brother. This girl is crazy. She had on some skin-tight high waist cut up shorts that stopped at the knee and some Gucci sneakers and a Gucci top, hoodie and headband to match. Did I mention the purse? The girl could dress her ass off.

"I cannot wait to see Niko today girl hopefully we can clear the air and get back on track like we were before."

I know my brother, he doesn't like surprises, but hopefully, he is at least nice to Faith it would crush her if he wasn't.

We make it to the visitation area waiting for his name to be called so we can know what window to head to. This place was all too familiar for me going up here to see my homies and my little niggas locked down. But I never wanted to be here for my brother, and he supposes to be untouchable he supposes to be our superman.

Niko Grant

"That's it girl let's go see your man," I tell Faith playfully. She was prob more excited than me.

We wait patiently at the window waiting for him to come on the other side.

When he comes out, he looks like a completely different person. This isn't my slim handsome little brother. This little nigga was huge!

He smiling ear to ear with his handsome self. I see why Faith loved my brother so much the nigga was finer than fine. Beautiful light brown eyes to accent his deep chocolate skin just like our daddy. Perfect teeth you would think he had braces with his chiseled jawline and deep dimples. My brother had it going even in jail. Hair cut was fresh as hell. I didn't understand. He had a taper on the sides and the back with the curved part on the top of his left side.

"What's the deal, Sissy! You finally coming to see a nigga huh? "

"What that shit do little bro! You know I been running around with your nephew, he has been driving me crazy. You see I brought Faith say hi Niko damn!"

He cut me an evil stare and nodded his head her way.

"Wassup Faith, how are you doing?"

She lit up with excitement that he even acknowledged her and grabbed the phone.

"Hey Niko, I know we having talked in a minute, but I missed you, and I wanted to see how you were doing.

Are you okay?"

This broad turn into complete mush when my brother is around, in the streets, she is the rowdiest out of the girls in the set. But when she around this nigga she try to be prim and proper.

"I'm good Faith, I appreciate you coming and everything."

I know when my brother super mad cause the nigga gets calm and then lets you have it most politely.

"But you know my girl wouldn't appreciate this shit you and my sister trying to pull making it seem like we got something going on and we don't."

With a shrug of his shoulders, he then let her have it. "Shit I coulda saw you when I got out hanging around the set quite frankly. Isn't that what you like to do? hang around my homies?"

Damn, he had to go there. Faith mouth drops, and she was stuck for a second.

"Niko you know after you I never talked to nobody else in the hood!" She yelped in desperation. He just shook his head and put his hand up, dismissing anything else she had to say.

"Aye look blood, I don't know SHIT! I know what I saw in the video of you blowing off the homie, and I ain't got shit else to say to you. I don't hate you, you feel me? I mean you my sister-friend you cool, but I don't fuck with you like that I got a girl."

Faith dropped the phone. Sad and heartbroken, she walked back into the waiting area.

"Damn Niko why you had to get at her like that I told you that video was old and he was hating cause you got his old bitch," I tell him trying to have her back, I mean she did give me a ride up here.

"I don't wanna hear that shit Nakea! Don't bring nobody up here but my momma and my girl period!" I rolled my eyes, and I told y'all that bitch got my brother thinking she his family.

"Whatever Niko, so what's up with this case?" I haven't been talking to his Lawyer because Carissa been paying for her and she gave strict instructions to the lady to only speak to her.

"Man I should be coming home tomorrow, I'm trying to surprise my girl my co-defendant taking the wrap for the burner and everything, so I'm just gone do community service and be on probation since this my first offense."

I was so happy, I couldn't wait to have my brother back in this field running shit.

"Good because Tmac and them not doing nothing right, and we need you back letting them niggas know who is who. They allowing every Hollywood nigga with some fame claim the hood so they can be at the club."

He looked at me disappointed and irritated I guess he wasn't trying to hear the shit I was talking about.

"Man you need to grow the fuck up! I ain't trying to be wrapped up in the shit look where I'm at? You love daddy so much, that nigga dead because he loved the block more than us!"

How dare he bring up our daddy like that.

"Don't say that Niko, daddy loved us!"

" Yeah that nigga loved us, but he loved the set more and the set ain't my responsibility I got my own family to be here for, Rissa having my baby."

What the fuck? I'm so glad Faith left to the waiting room she would be curled up on the floor if she heard him say that.

"What do you mean, she is having yo baby?"

"Sissy, what the fuck it sounds like? She got pregnant and be quiet don't tell mama ima tell her when I come home. And I don't wanna hear that you fucking with my girl. I ain't gone have it."

I roll my eyes again, I should never come to see this nigga. He is the bearer of bad news, talking about Carissa pregnant; she gonna be acting like we unworthy of being around the damn baby. How he knows it's his anyway, he's been in jail almost four months.

**Two more minutes inmates **

The officer says them behind the glass.

"Alright sissy, I gotta go. I don't want you to think I don't love you cause I do. I want you to grow up my nephew doesn't need to be around this shit you like. Try moving or something."

My brother loved me, and I appreciated it, but I'm the big sister he doesn't get to tell me a Muthafuckin thing.

" Yeah, Cj daddy said he put some money in yo books too by the way."

"Yeah I know I talked to him last night, he told me he

fucking with Kiani now, they engaged and all that.... if you still trying to fuck with that nigga leave him alone, he doesn't want you like that anymore. I told you to stop acting so ghetto."

Oh, this little nigga had me messed up!

"Bye Niko damn! I love you annoying little boy."

"Bye, sissy give me a kiss!"

One more minute inmate!

The jailer says again. This time in an irritated tone.

"Mauh!"

I hang up the phone, wave, and watch as he walks out of view then head towards the waiting area. That's where I spot Faith sitting down looking sad, and face red from crying and humiliation. We didn't say much to each other cause she can tell knowing my brother and the dumb look I had on my face he let me have it too.

I couldn't believe that Cavi was engaged with that bitch Kiani. What did he see in her that he didn't see in me? Faith and I were the baddest redbones in the city, and you couldn't tell us anything, everybody wanted us. Except the niggas that we wanted to want us I guess.

If he loved her so much why did he slept with me last week? I mean I didn't make it hard for him to have access to me because we are a family and I thought no matter what I was number one. But this home-wrecking bitch took my nigga, and he thinks I'm about to let him have her around my baby? Hell the fuck no! I do not think so.

I pull out my phone and send him one of the many messages he will get from now on regarding seeing his son.

ME: I don't feel comfortable with you having your little Fiancé around my baby overnight. So if you want to see My baby you gotta come over here!

Not even a min later I get a reply

BABYDADDY: Bitch wtf you think you about to play baby games because you in your feelings cause we not together, and I moved on, you got another thing coming!

Let the games begin.

Chapter 10
Miranda Beal

"Juju, hurry up in the bathroom, you take longer than me damn! ... ain't I suppose to be the girly girl in this relationship?"

Today was the day if Judith little work best friend baby shower. Ever since our little altercation, I stay out of their small business. I'm not the type of girlfriend who likes to mix friends anyway. So as long as no more funny shit was going on, their friendship was fine by me.

The girl Taylor has appointed Judith the God mom and boy has she took her title seriously. She has our living room filled with baby presents from bathtubs to baby strollers. According to Judith, the girl doesn't have that much family, and Judith has taken it upon herself to take her under her wing.

"Alright bae lets go, I know you ain't feeling Tay like that but that's my homie I want y'all to get along."

I didn't want to hear that shit she was talking about. You know how stud bitches like to play stepdaddy to females babies, and I feel like that's what she was trying to do.

"Where is her baby daddy at anyway? Why you buy all this shit?" I ask as I put on my sandals ready to head out the door.

"Some dude named Jeremy, she been dating since high school; and he goes to your school too you may know him!"

Wait, this might be the girl that Makenzie was talking about. What am I suppose to do right now? Do I tell Kenz I'm on my way to her nigga baby shower? We finally load the car and head to North Long Beach to the baby shower location. I'm on high alert, praying this ain't the Jeremy or the girl that my friend has been talking about this whole time.

Judith is first to get out the car, warmly welcomed by the few family members of Taylor's.

"Juju what that shit do girl!" A hippie-looking curly head chick says from the porch. Judith comes in for a big hug and walks her towards the car.

"Raine this is my girl Miranda, Miranda this is Taylor's cousin Raine." I step out of the car and welcome her with a friendly wave and church hug, then initiated getting some of these gifts out of the car.

Once we arrived at the backyard, we spotted Taylor. The sight of us coming in with so many gifts made her burst into tears. She hobbled over to Judith, giving her the biggest hug a person could give with a belly in the way. She then came towards me and said.

"Thank you for being open to our friendship, and this is one of the closest friends I have. I know that our first encounter wasn't the best. But I'm grateful for your willingness to allow us to continue a friendship."

Aww wow, she was so lovely. I immaturely wanted to dislike her because of our first time meeting at the hospital. But they haven't done anything too fishy to have me suspect that anything was going on between her and Ju. I welcome her with a hug and find seating at a nearby table. I'm not social like most of my other friends I'm more reserved and to myself. So, I'm feeling hella uncomfortable at this baby shower while Judith's happy ass was running around like she was the baby daddy doing all the hosting for the games and the raffles.

Wait a minute, where is the baby daddy? Judith said that his name was Jeremy and he went to my school. I have a feeling it's the Jeremy that's giving my girl Makenzie the blues making her look crazy on campus. At this point, I'm just staying on high alert for any familiar faces.

An hour into the shower in comes Jeremy, damn I was hoping this wasn't going to be his baby shower, now I gotta tell Makenzie this shit. He comes brushing his whack ass fade heading straight to Taylor who just pushed him away. He looked as if he was pleading with her, attempting to kiss her on the forehead when I heard her say.

"Just leave Mac, your late, your drunk I'm trying to enjoy myself go!" Jeremy wasn't trying to hear that though, and soon her little family including Judith ass circled them to get some resolution. I can hear Jeremy pleading his case in a slurred drunken voice to the family.

"Talk to me in the house, please! Please! I cannot do this with you out here." The nigga was drunk which is not surprising he always drinking.

I didn't know what Makenzie saw in him. He was handsome no doubt, chocolate skin, nice teeth, and a too cool for school demeanor about him. But, he wasn't the type of guy my girl would normally date. He was short, he wasn't athletic, and he was always drunk, high or something in the middle.

I continued to sit and observe the spectacle that has become of this girl's baby shower. After a couple more moments of pleading to Taylor on Jeremy's end, he finally got her to go inside the house to speak with him. I used that time to text Makenzie and told her what was going on.

ME: Girl... I'm at the Taylor girl baby shower, and its confirmed girl it's Jeremy's baby.

MAKENZIE: smh. I had a feeling, girl. I just had an abortion and he having a baby shower. I feel so fucking stupid.

Woah, she didn't tell me that before. I didn't even know what to say. I immediately walked over to Judith letting her know I was ready to go. I can't sit here any longer and support this sick shit.

.

Chapter 11
Kiani Storm

"Ugh! This is so frustrating why can't we pick him up Cavi?"

It was spring break and Carter, and I was planning to take his son Cj to Disney Land for the week. Baby Carter and I have built our very own unique relationship, and I am crazy about that little munchkin. I had already packed all of our bags and purchased our matching shirts for our pictures. I don't get what happened. Before a couple weeks ago I was hanging with little Cj every other day. Cavi wasn't just a weekend dad, but he was involved. Picked his baby up from daycare, we had flashcards, letters, blocks, and all the learning supplies to have him in tip-top shape ready for school this upcoming fall.

"Man, his momma, been tripping, I guess she feels a way because she sees how serious me and you are. Man, don't even worry about it imma figure this shit out."

Carter hasn't been the same since he hasn't been able to pick up his baby as frequently as he liked. He was more grumpy and ready to pop off about anything out of place. I've been trying to relieve that stress by having dinner ready when he gets home and giving him massages. But nothing I do will replace him wanting his baby.

My thing is, I don't get why all of a sudden, she tripping that we be in a relationship. We've been in a relationship, and what changed a couple of weeks ago?

"Well, we can, at least, hit up Roscoe's as planned, Cj would have been so excited to get him a waffle huh bae?"

Carter was pressing so hard on his phone. I thought that he would break the screen. He was irritated that today was supposed to be the start of an amazing spring break, and his baby momma ruined it.

I ain't never met the girl before like I said Cavi don't have no around anything that has to do with the hood, and apparently, hood is her middle name.

I mean I have seen pics of her before. She was cute, but she damn sure wasn't me. Really fair complexion black girl with two full sleeves going up both arms of random cartoon characters and niggas names. She was one of those pretty ghetto girls that took the shit too far, and now they damn near look rough.

She just didn't fit into the image Carter is going for now. He and his friends were putting the money together to open a new barbershop in Hawthorne and we've been shopping around for townhomes and condos in the El Segundo and Torrance areas.

My cosmetics line was doing better than ever, and my insta paid advertisements were bringing in some big money, we were pretty well off. Carter needed a lady to compliment his style and grace, not some hood rat like her.

"Haha yeah, baby that's a good idea, some Roscoes in his honor shit."

He said with a smirk, the thought of that little boy lights up my man's face.

"Then I could maybe drop him a waffle off on the way home. Let's go."

❧

We get to the Roscoe's on Pico and are seated in the back at the booth area. I'm starving, stomach growling, ready to eat at this point. The waiter finally comes, and I order my regular Obama Special with a waffle and a sunrise. Carter's weird self gets chicken and fries at a waffle place. Isn't that crazy? Anyway, we were waiting for our order, talking about our change in plans for the upcoming week.

"So, shit man, I guess if we ain't gone hit Disneyland, you might; we'll go on that girl's trip with Makenzie and then to Palm Springs... shit, I don't know how you feel baby."

I did want to go on that trip with the girls; I don't get to see them as much as they see each other being that we go to a different school. I bet I'm missing out on a whole ton of tea right now too.

"Yeah, I think imma go ahead and go with them to Palm Springs and we can reschedule the Disneyland trip for sometime this summer or something."

Suddenly, Carter looks up, and it was if he has seen a ghost. Whoever he was looking at was behind me, so I played it cool until they walked up alongside me to see who it was.

"Daddddddyyyyyyy!"

It was little Cj, he dashed to his daddy side of the booth dangling from Cavi's neck.

"Wassup little man?! I miss you so much .... you miss daddy?"

"Yeah, I miss you, Hi Kee Kee!" He looks over at me face lighting up with glee.

" Hi, poppa bear come give me a hug!" He starts for my side of the booth, but before he could get there a voice says firmly to him.

"Uhhh huh CJ, don't go talking to strangers that are with your daddy! Come on we got our table to sit at!"

Grabbing his arm immediately and directing him towards the booth right next to ours that sat two other people.

"That's Kee Kee mommy! And I wanna sit with my daddy and Kee pleaseeee."

Cavi was furious, and I was confused. I knew that LA was small but damn, what are the odds that me and his baby momma in the same restaurant sitting one booth from each other.

He was boiling, he turned around to the booth behind us and told the baby momma.

"Aye cuh, what you even doing here my nigga? And if my son wanna sit with me and my lady, then he can. She ain't no Muthafuckin stranger."

I'm sitting in a position facing her booth, and I watch and observe as they go back and forth.

"Nigga who are you trying to go big on? I don't know that bitch, and I don't want her around my son! Period! You wanna be engaged and not tell me. Fuck You, Carter Kentrell Thompson!"

Oh, that's what she mad about. I take a glance at my left hand and fiddle with my engagement ring.

Damn ring, you sure causing a lot of trouble around here.

"Calm down Nakea, Cj doesn't need to see you going off like this." A chick at her table tells her in a mild-mannered tone.

"Fuck this let's go... come on Cj mommy is going to bring you to get a waffle another time okay?" Looking at Cj, I could tell that he wasn't going to make it easy for her.

"Nooo! I'm staying with my daddy and Kee Kee today." Running to our booth hopping in his daddy's lap.

"Fuck is your problem Nakea! My son can stay with me if he wants to. I don't even know why you are testing me on hood!"

She gets up from her booth and walks to ours, hovering over CJ and Cavi. "TESTING YOU?! You played me I been here all these years not this black ass bitch!" pointing at me.

I'm not one for confrontation, and my nigga right here anyway imma let him speak up for me.

"You are that jealous; you are trying to make a scene like some RAT up in this restaurant."

That triggered something for her. "RAT? I got your fucking rat!"

She dashed towards me and grabbed my hair. Everything after that was all chaos. I'm grabbing her hair as well as trying to uppercut her in the face. The syrup is all over the floor, and the booths and tables are all miss arranged.

Waiters have jumped in the tussle, trying to pry our hands out of each other's hair. They finally got us apart and grabbed her escorting her out first.

"Yeah, bitch! I bet he gonna leave yo ass just like he left me! Fuck you Cavi!!!" She yells with tears flowing down her cheeks, and her face flustered with rage.

Carter was holding crying Cj, trying to console him as he cried hysterically.

"I got something for you, Bitch! You ain't about to get away with this shit none!"

He walks towards me, but I stop him dead in his tracks.

"Cavi just take me home."

Chapter 12
Makenzie Gray

"Palm Springs bitches!" Travis Porter Bring it Back playing in the background as we pull up to our vacation rental.

♫ *Run and hit that p**** like a crash dummy*
Bend it over, touch ya toes
*Shake that a** for me*
Bounce that a on the flo,' bring it back up
Hit a split on the dick, shawty act up ♫

"Aye!! Get it God mommy," Carissa yells through video chat to Kiani twerking in that car. Rissa was bigger than ever now, and it was no way that she was going to be able to keep up with us on this trip. Hell, with Niko being home we haven't seen much of her ass anyway.

It was spring break, and we were ready to turn up. All the drama I had going on with Jeremy, I was prepared to leave all that behind. Miranda hit me up last week telling me she had eyes on him at Judith's coworker Taylor's baby shower, and his petty ass was the baby daddy! When I approached him about it he told me that he hadn't known me long enough, so he didn't owe me that information — the nerve of him, and to top it off. We had another falling out because I didn't give him my ATM pin to make him some money. Like I was born at night, but not last night! I know the trend was to finesse these girls by fucking up their bank account. It wasn't gonna be me, that's for damn sure.

I've been planning this getaway for us gals for a while now, and with all that's going on in everyone's life, it is much needed.

"I'm so glad I decided to come on the trip instead of staying home with Carter. His baby momma got me stressed the hell out!"

Kiani yells from the backseat in between taking shots of her bottle of plain Ciroc. My girl fucked around and got a nigga with a crazy baby momma that was giving them the straight blues.

"Since the fight last week I ain't been saying shit to him! I'm Kiani fucking Storm! Period! You think imma be fighting bitches over you?!"

My girl was gonna off the Ciroc. Kiani was normally calm about everything, but being forced into a fight pushed her over the edge. She did not like confrontation at all. She didn't even like it when we called her out on flaking on everything. But this week, we were going to forget about all the drama and have some fun.

Once we arrived at our vacation rental, the girls were amazed.

"You outdid yourself with this one Kenz," Judith says looking at the vacation house as she grabs the bags out of the trunk. Yeah, we let Judith go on the girl trip even though she is a spouse. No spouses allowed has always been the rule, but we always make exceptions for Juju.

The rental was the bomb, three pink houses on one compound with a pool filled with some dollar, flamingo, and unicorn floaties with a basketball court in the middle. You couldn't tell me a damn thing, I think I just knew I was a world renounced travel agent in my past life or something.

"So, what's the plan y'all, what are we doing tonight?" Kiani was too ready to turn up, but after all that driving, I just wanted to unpack and recoup.

"Girl, I'm not about to play with yo lit ass! We need to go to the grocery store so we can BBQ and make drinks." I yell from the bedroom in the main house. I don't know why I rented this big as a compound for just four of us, but it was the bomb, and I wanted to do it for the gram with these pictures this weekend.

"Alright, well, let's get ready to go right now, half the day has already gone from the drive," Judith says sitting by the pool while Miranda unpacks her clothes. The way she was talking about unpacking you would think she would be doing her shit.

"Okay cool then, come on y'all let's find a grocery store out here."

∽

We all hop in the car and find a Grocery store ten minutes away from our rental.

"We need some smoothie in a bag mix you know I love my drinks smoothie-like," I say heading towards the frozen section.

"Bitch! You gonna turn into a fucking smoothie! Head ass" Kiani yells from the end of the aisle. Oh, yea I forgot to mention, Kiani talks big shit when she's drunk.

"Shut yo drunk ass up, hoe, we are on a mission," Miranda says while grabbing some smoothie bags out of the freezer.

"A mission for what ?!" She yells while opening a bag of hot chips, eating them as she walks down the aisle.

"Embarrassing," Miranda says, trying to be goody-two-shoes while Judith is here. But, shes' gonna be right on Kiani level by tonight.

We separate and grab all the food and drinks we planned on using for the weekend and met back at the register. Palm Springs looks like a straight retirement area with all the older white men and women staring at us throughout the store like they never have seen black girls before.

"Well, hello there ladies, looks like your on vacation," this old wrinkled white man says as he rings up his groceries in front of us in the self check out register.

"Yeah spring break, we been working hard in school time to have fun," Miranda says I'm her corporate voice, she was quick to code-switch.

"Well, that's beautiful! Back in my days, my wife and I weren't able to go to many places on vacation together because she was a black woman, and I'm white." He looked away as his eyes watered.

"You gals are so full of life I've been hearing you all around the store I want to go ahead and pay for your items so you all can have a good time."

"Oh sir, you don't have to do that, we can purchase our items" I blurted out, I wasn't a fan of being nobody's charity case. Kiani gripped me on the shoulder in a failed whisper.

"Bitch, let your pride go and allow someone to be nice to you." Followed by jumping on the old man's lap, giving him a big hug.

"Ohhh, thank you Santa sir. You truly are a blessing!"

Miranda almost passed out with embarrassment grabbing Kiani by the arm.

"Girl get yo ass up off this man... I'm so sorry sir as you can see she started the party early."

"Oh haha, sweetheart, it's fine go ahead and ring up the items, bills on Santa."

As we headed back to the house, I told the girls all about the plans I had for us for the days to come. Kiana had control of the Aux and acted as the Dj until she abruptly turned off the music.

Judith had had enough and leaned into the front seat and gave Kiani a cold stare. "Stormy turn the music back on bro, you tripping."

"Girl, leave me alone, I got something to say!"

Miranda playfully rolled her eyes, "what you got to say stormy?"

Kiani put her hand to her face in a playful motion as if she was thinking about it.

"Ummmm...I'm just playing., but for real though, I think we need to have an intervention with Makenzie y'all."

"With me? What the heck is wrong with me" this caught me completely off guard. Kiani looked over to me with a hurt in her eyes.

"Your so beautiful and have a heart of gold, always wanting to do something for somebody, why don't you think you deserve somebody nice to you just because?"

Damn, I never thought about my life in that context.

"I allow you guys to do nice stuff for me all that time. what are you talking about?"

Miranda jumped in before Kiani could reply.

"She was talking about a man Kenz, you almost had us miss out all this free shit."

I jumped in quick,

"Cause, what did he want from us in return, ain't shit free men are users."

Kiani saw this conversation was getting tense and attempted to defuse the situation.

"All I'm saying is, allow someone to be nice to you. You deserve that much."

The rest of the ride to the house was a moment of reflection. The car was loud, and my girls were bumping music, but to me, it was a silent ride. I thought about how in every relationship I've been in. I find myself giving everything I could, and always seeming to come short of the needs of my partner in their eyes.

That being the reasoning why I was not given the love I and affection, I craved from them in return.

My friends were right, and it was time that I allow a man to step in and be a man and stop trying to convince a nigga of why I worth it.

As we arrive at the rental house, I notice a white Mercedes Benz in the driveway.

"Oh, shit y'all that Carter ... what the fuck is he doing here?!"

Kiani straightened the hell up real quick, and she checked herself out in the visor mirror reapplied her smeared lipstick and hopped out the car like she was with the bullshit.

She sassily switched her hips over to Carter's car. Putting her hands in the driver window all in his face.

"What the hell you doing here, Cavi? This is a girl trip!"

"Oh shit, it's about to go down y'all," Judith dirty ass says in the backseat of the car. Miranda and I say nothing, and we were enjoying Kiani act crazy for once and let her hair down.

Carter gets out of the car and wraps his arms around Kiani whispering in her ear, kissing her all over her face. The shit was pretty cute if I say so myself.

"Move, don't kiss me! ... I'm mad at you," you can hear her voice softening up. Fucking sucker. There goes our girl trip.

"Come get the groceries out of the car since you are crashing my damn trip!" Now, Kiani wants to act like she still tuff. We already know she's not mad anymore.

"Alright baby whatever you want, come on bro, we gonna stay with them."

Suddenly, a guy gets out of the passenger seat and walks towards the car.

"Waddup queen, pop the trunk real quick so I can get the shit out the back."

This nigga was fine ass fuck, where does Carter get these homies from?

He had smooth caramel skin with a broad frame as if he played football — pearly white teeth with dark brown hair with a clean fade and a goatee.

He was Carter's friend by the attire, he was a very bright dresser. He was wearing a short-sleeve Burberry button up and some shorts to match with some all-white forces.

I smile politely and popped the trunk.

"Aye sis what that shit do, sorry for crashing y'all trip. Here's a little something for the inconvenience."

Carter handed me a wad of cash, and I looked back a Miranda with a smirk.

"We in the money bishhhhh"

I get out of the car and go to the trunk to get a bag.

"Aye, what you doing mama I said I was getting them." Carter's friend says walking back from sitting some bags on the porch.

"I just thought I could help that's all," I say in response.

"You fucking with a real man. Go sit yo pretty ass down in the house and relax I got you."

"We... Well okay," I was caught off guard; he was so straight forward, but I liked it.

Maybe having some guys at the girl trip wouldn't be so bad.

Chapter 13
Niko Grant

A nigga was finally home, and you couldn't tell me shit. I had my girl and my baby on the way. All I had to do next was make these money plays to get us the fuck from around my family

When I was down Carissa was working doubles and doing nails on the side, making sure I had money on my books and money to pay the lawyer fees. When I touched down my big bro, Carter handed me a stack and gave it right to Carissa; told her all that working was out. All I want her to do is to focus on school right now, and maybe do that nail shit for fun if she feels like it.

My ratchet ass sister came to see me when I was locked down and brought that rat Faith with her. Faith and I were together for a cool min when Carissa and I had broken up. She claims she was pregnant by me, but every time I turned around, she was in one of the homies faces — all in the pictures throwing up the set.

Who wants that girl on that bull shit? Not me, so I dropped that bitch and got my back Rissa back.

Faith got an exclusive hold on my family because she's a rat-like them and wants to be in the face all the time. Carissa ain't ever gave a fuck about being all in the face cause she knows that ain't the shit I'm trying to be on.

It was my first night out with my homies, and we found ourselves in the strip club.

♫ *Round of applause, baby make that ass clap, drop it to the floor, make that ass clap* ♫

"Aye nigga! You back home. It's good to have you back bro!" Carter yells over the loud music at Diamonds Strip Club.

This was the hottest strip club in LA. And I and my homies are them niggas, so our section was packed with strippers and females who wanted our bottle or wanted to be seen.

My boy Verified on the turntables tonight gave me a shout out after the last song.

"We welcoming my sandbox dawg Niko aka Meechie home tonight! Everybody turn up let's go!

We turned up at the club for about an hour after that. Throwing money all over the place the shit was going up.

The night was early, but we are never the type of niggas to get caught slipping nowhere, so we made sure we headed out that bitch a little before it was over.

"What's the next move bro?! I'm trying to hit the after hours!" I wasn't ready to go home, shit I been locked down for months.

We hopped in my elevated blacked out Jeep Wrangler, and Cavi gives me a serious stare.

"So nigga, what's yo plan now that you're home. Can't be on all that wild shit like before, you got a seed on the way."

Carter didn't give a damn that this was my first time at a function since being home. While all the homies have a great time, I was about to get a lecture.

"Bro I'm good! I'm back I'm yo right hand you already know this."

"Nah, I don't need you to be my right hand anymore." He said is in a serious cold tone.

"Bruh, what the fuck do you mean? I got a kid on the way; I need to make this money to start me up." I don't know what this nigga was talking about, but I need to pass one more time. A nigga felt like I was being fired or something.

"Man, I ain't trying to hustle no more Meechie, we gotta clean this money and be done with this shit."

I gave an exasperated huff in the air. "What are you trying to do bro?"

Whatever he was trying to do it better insure we getting paid. I can't allow my girl to work overtime for us ever again. When I went down I was low and desperate trying to make a quick pass before going legit and working for the oil refinery.

But to keep it real, fuck working them long as slave hours. I'm trying to make my bread and have some time to enjoy my shit.

" Nigga let's open a barbershop, you always cutting niggas hair anyway. Shit, you just did my line up for this party." Cavi's eyes lit up like two light bulbs just flashed before his eyes.

"Alright bro, so we gotta go back to school for this shit?!" He knew damn well I didn't fuck with being in a boring ass class.

"Yeah man, but we got money to open up our shop and can clean our money. We gotta have some shit to leave to our kids' bro, and I just don't feel right about this street shit anymore."

I think my sister stressing Cavi out threating him with court and shit was enough to have the nigga wanna change his life. What judge is going to grant joint custody to a nigga that slang for a living?

"Alright bro, but I can't be broke going through no fucking school, in the meantime, we gotta do whatever we gotta do."

Niggas like us were already known for the niggas with baddest bitches and the flyest gear. Now, we gonna be the niggas giving out the flyest cuts.

"Nigga, we gotta hustle for this shop money, and we gotta make our girls a shop and shit right next door."

Cavi always had the master plans, and if his plans made since I was fucking with it. Before he was my sister's baby daddy, he's been my best friend since the sandbox.

He the only person that can tell me about the dumb shit I be on and listen.

Suddenly I hear a knock at the window. Hand to our pistols we look over at the back window and see a female silhouette.

"Aye who the fuck at my window!"

"It's me Meechie, open the door baby."

I knew that voice from anywhere, and it was Faith dumb ass. I groan irritably and unlock the car door.

"Hey Cavi, Ummm, hey Meech what y'all doing in the parking lot still? y'all left the club a while ago."

"Man...how you know when you left the club? Have you been stalking us cuh? Carter looks back at her skeptically.

I don't trust Faith like that, and it was a time when I thought she was gone be my rider. But when I was just locked down, I heard all about how she was going from homie to homie in the neighborhood. Shit that only fueled my reasoning on why I'll never fuck with her again. I don't want any bitch that hangs out more than me on some ghetto shit.

"Naw not even! What the fuck, I work here muthafucka." See that's what the fuck I'm talking about working at a strip club — fucking rat.

"What do you want, Faith?" I want her to get out of my fucking car.

"Can y'all give me a ride home?"

"Blooooooood, catch a Uber, my nigga, fuck you been doing to get home from work?"

"Just, please! I wouldn't ask you if I didn't need a ride. Niko, don't do me like that."

"Man alright don't pull no messy shit either trying to message my bitch cause I'll donkey Kong yo shit Faith on my momma."

She rolled her eyes with a mischievous smirk on her face.

"Aye nigga drop me off before you take her home ... I don't want no parts cuh, and yo sister already had my shit fucked up."

Man, this nigga gone have it look worst for me, I only said yeah cause he with me.

I look over at this nigga Carter in desperation. He looks over at me blankly, like he doesn't give a fuck about what he knows I'm trying to say without actually saying.

"What nigga? I ain't fucking with it cuh drop me off."

"Maannnnn. Alright, I'm gonna drop you off at Nana house bro."

"Man what? Take me home cuh!." I look at him like he's stupid and mouth slowly.

"Shut The Fuck Up" and nodded my head towards the back seat.

I didn't want Faith to know where my nigga stayed so she can tell my sister. Carter's grandma Nana's house was fair game for all of us growing up, so it didn't matter.

"Oh, shit... alright bro, good looking." He says finally coming to realize what I was trying to do.

Faith poped her ole water bottle head ass in between me and Carter and looks at us both.

"You know I can hear y'all right? What y'all don't want me to see? All these years I can't know where you stay bro?"

Carter bops her playfully on her forehead, pushing her back into the backseat.

"Hell naw Faith, with your dirty ass. You and yo crazy ass bestie not gone terrorize my private residents cuh."

Faith rolls her eyes in annoyance. She's so nosy, she hated not being in some shit.

"Whatever nigga, Meechie drop Rockhead off so you can take me home." As she pops Carter in the back of the head.

⚲

"Alright bro, see you later. Don't be on no bull shit Faith." Carter says as he gets out of my car and heads towards the front gate Nana's house.

"Bye, fool! Tell my nana I said hi and I miss her." Faith yells out the window as she attempts to hop in the front seat of my car.

Carter waved Faith off in annoyance and goes inside the house.

I push her back into the backseat before she can get both feet in towards the front.

"What the fuck is you doing my nigga? Stay yo ass in the backseat blood, pretend this a taxi ride."

"Damn why are you acting like I can't sit with you? You were my nigga for years period. Now, you treat me like some jump-off."

Here she goes with this shit, don't get me wrong I didn't hate the girl. To keep it real with y'all, a nigga got love for her. However, a nigga knows when he can grow further as a man with his woman company or not. And fucking with Faith, I'll be on the front of an airbrushed shirt.

"Just sit back my nigga. We almost to yo house."

As I'm driving, I keep feeling something touch my ears, and I hear a sudden shutter sound from a camera. I turn around to peep her bring her foot by my headrest.

"What the fuck is are you doing bro, you taking pictures of me, my nigga?!"

"No, I'm not Meechie. I promise baby." She says in a conniving tone.

"I'm not your nigga anymore, you blew with the hood rat shit... Man, we are at yo house get yo ass the fuck out my car blood."

She grabs her stuff and swings open my back door. She followed by reaching back in the car and slapping me in the face.

Poww

"Fuck you Niko you know I love you, and you treat me like we never had anything! Having a baby with this fucking girl! Acting like my baby didn't exist!" Tears rolling down her face uncontrollably.

Damn man, I didn't mean to make her cry. I still got a soft spot for Faith. I've known her since we were kids and we were together growing up before I met Rissa.

I hop out of the car and grab her up by her shoulders.

"Look, man come here." I try to be compassionate as I can so I can get her dumb ass to listen.

"I got a lot of love for you, I know you carried my baby, but we are no longer together. It didn't work out, and I want this shit with me and Carissa to work."

She turned her face to block me from seeing her tears fall. I grab her chin and make her look at me.

" Look at me bro. You gotta grow up. And even if you don't, you deserve a nigga to meet you where you at and want to be with you. That ship has sailed with me and you though Faith I'm sorry."

She gazed in my eyes with what looks like an ounce of hope that I may kiss her or take her in the house to dick her down. But I was cool on her and her bull shit for real.

"Ma, give me a hug and go to the house. It's late."

I reach out to hug her and she pushed me away.

" No it's okay I'm cool, you gonna regret not fucking choosing me in the end that square bear bitch can't do nothing for you that I can do!" As she stormed away, heading towards her apartment building.

I hop back in the whip and zoom off. I tried to be nice about the shit.

Some people are and will always be a part of your history, but not a part of your destiny.

Chapter 14
Parker Little

"Pass thaaa bluntttt Parks," Mac says to me as we sit in my car bumping the Nipsey The Marathon mixtape. My baby Mac loved Nipsey you couldn't tell him anything when it came to him.

It was the top of the morning, and he was vibing to his favorite track IDGAf when he got a call from his baby mom Taylor. She was trying to schedule an appointment for her final ultrasound and needed his availability.

I wasn't tripping off of him having a baby on the way because her pregnancy happened before we got serious. And anyway he practically lives at my house. All of his toiletries some of his clothes are hung up in my closet, the only time I know about him seeing Taylor is when it's for the baby.

When Jeremy hung up the phone, he looked over at me, grabbed my face and planted a big kiss on my lips and forehead. I loved it when he did that it was so cute.

"You know what I love about you, Parker."

I smiled and take a hit of the blunt and say to him playfully. "No I don't know, why don't you tell me."

"When we spend time together, your not worried about anyone else but me and you. I love that about you, Parker." He says while taking the blunt out of my hand and hitting it.

He was right I wasn't worried about nobody else anymore not even that stupid ass bitch Makenzie. He made it clear to me that they were no longer, and I didn't have to deal with her antics anymore.

I open the car door, and a cloud a smoke escapes. It's time for me to get ready for my long day ahead.

"Aye baby, let me drop you off on campus today I need to run some errands," Jeremy says while dumping the ashes and tobacco from the blunt outside.

"Okay, let me get my stuff packed and get dressed

for class."

I quickly head into the house to get ready for class. I took my time doing my makeup and hair because I had a lunch date with the homegirl and didn't want anyone seeing me look crazy on campus.

"Alright, you ready Parker? You're going to be late if you don't hurry up!" Jeremy yells from the living room sofa.

I head towards the living room while slinging my backpack across my shoulder.

"Don't you have class today, Mac?"

"No, my professor canceled class, so I'm living leisure today for sure." While laying back on the couch and widening his legs like he was relaxing on a beach.

I chuckle at his dramatics. " Well get up Mac cause you have to drop me off. Not all of us could be so lucky."

⚬

After class, I had lunch with my girl Morgan at the cafe on campus.

Morgan was on the school's volleyball team. She was

the shortest one but packed the most punch. All the black guys on campus wanted her because she was short, light complexion and thicker than a jar of peanut butter. She didn't show to much interest in them though she was head over hills for Steven Rolley, the starting guard on the basketball team.

"So, what's going on with you sista? You still dating Jeremy?"

She loved to be all in my business. I just laughed and shared it all.

"Yeah, girl! We practically live together right now, most of his stuff is at my place, and he is there every night."

"What about Makenzie?" I instantly got defensive.

"What about her, we saw her a couple of weeks ago, and he walked right past her, and didn't say a word. She's no longer a factor in our lives."

Morgan threw her hands up, surrendering to my confident statement.

"Hold on there, girl! Well, excuse me." Laughing while taking a sip of her green smoothie.

I didn't care what nobody thought, I love me some

Jeremy, and I know he loves me. Shit has been going pretty good lately, and I was on cloud 9.

One of my siblings, my little brother Keith did not like him at all.

He and Jeremy have had multiple encounters at some of my family events, and my brother barely shakes his hand.

After that fight at the basketball house, I didn't come around my family until the wounds healed. I didn't want to have to tell them the full details of what happened.

Keith was my half-sibling that I was closest to because we lived in the same city and were only a couple months apart. My brother's mom made sure we spent a lot of time together growing up.

He was tall and buff in comparison to my short and tiny frame. Had a vanilla complexion, pink pout lips, almond-shaped brown eyes and wore that stupid hair cut with the taper around and sponge brush curly thing at the top.

I also had a half-sibling who is not far in age, my sister Faith. She's hood famous in LA and lives a way faster life than me. We don't have anything in common. Because

Faith's mom was so into the hood life, my mom didn't allow me to spend time with her. So we don't speak, we only communicate rarely via social media. I know I could call her in any emergency like what happened at the basketball house. But I chose not to do that because people wouldn't have just been beaten up, they would've been dead.

An hour later, after some laughs and giggles with my girl Morgan, it was time for Jeremy to pick me up from campus.

I call him multiple times, but no answer.

"What the heck is going on he knows what time he was supposed to come."

It's starting to get late, my patience had run thin, and suddenly, I get a call from Jeremy.

"Where the hell are you Mac!" I answered the phone in rage, not even allowing him to say a word.

"Who is this that's been calling my child's father?" Woah, this can't be who I think it is.

"Ta... Taylor?" I ask in a state of confusion. I don't understand what's happening.

Suddenly I hear a distant sound of Jeremy in the

background

"Come on baby we gotta go I gotta drop you off at home before I pick the homeboy up from school."

He got this bitch in my fucking house and my car. That was his errands for today? I was livid, and nothing could calm me down at this point.

I yell in the phone, hoping he can some joe hear my voice in the background.

"You got that girl in my car and my house, Jeremy!?"

Suddenly I hear the phone hang up. When I try to call back, it was sent to voicemail each time.

It was settled; I was going to have to get my family involved. I immediately called my brother Keith.

"What that shit do sis?" I was so embarrassed to tell him I allowed a nigga to drive my car and stay at my house. I just started to cry.

"I need you to pick me up from campus," I say sniffling trying to stop the tears from rolling down my face.

"What you mean you need me to pick you up? Where is your car dude... you let that nigga drive it didn't you?" You could hear the irritation in his voice. But quite frankly I didn't give a fuck.

I didn't feel like going into details with him about what happened at the moment.

"Yeah Keith I did, you gone pick me up or not because if not I can just catch the bus."

I was so irritated, I never been one to ask for things because I always made sure I had my shit.

"Man, yeah I'm on my way up there right now don't trip sis I got you.

৵

"So, what happened?" Keith said as soon as I got into his all-black challenger.

"Dammit, Keith let me just regroup quickly," I say as I put on my seatbelt.

"Fuck all that Parker, where is this nigga in yo shit?" He turned the car off at the one-lane intersection on campus, holding traffic for all the cars behind us.

"He at my house with another girl Keith okay! Damn, can we go!"

His mouth dropped; he was so disappointed. Sometimes, I forget who is the older sibling with the way he reacts to things I tell him.

"Oh ... ok, bet then" Nodding his head slowly like he thinking up a master plan.

The drive to my house was quiet for a while. My brother was so mad and disappointed in me, and he didn't even want to talk to me.

Then suddenly, my phone rang, and it was Jeremy. I answer immediately.

"Where the hell are you?"

"Aye, who is it that nigga Mac calling you?... put that shit on speaker," Keith says, glancing over at me, holding the phone to my face. I put it on speaker and hear Jermey stumble over his words on what happened and why he has yet to pick me up from campus.

"I'm so sorry baby after running my errands I came home and went to sleep where are you on campus I'm on my way now." I couldn't believe this bastard was so comfortable telling this lie.

"Aye play cool don't argue with that nigga we on our way." My brother whispers as he speeds down the freeway to get off on Cherry.

I give a big huff into the air and play as cool as I can like my brother says.

"Yeah yeah, my brother picked me up, so I'll just meet you at home."

"I'm so sorry Parks! I was so sleepy, and I'll see you in a bit and make it up to you baby I promise."

This was the first time that I truly felt like he was pure bullshit. But my heart wanted me to believe that something had to be a misunderstanding.

"Man I know you not over there believing that bullshit Parker." It was like my brother was reading my mind. He and I both knew I was a sucker for this damn Jeremy.

We arrive at the house, and before I got out of the car, I told my brother not to come in the house, tripping off the bat; let's try to figure out if it was a misunderstanding or not.

He said he wouldn't do anything crazy, so we went into the house and Mac greeted us immediately.

"What's the deal bro!" Attempting to shake Keith's hang and come in for a hug but Keith stood cold with a stiff nod and sat down on the couch.

"Well damn, it's like that bro? What's up baby I'm so sorry." Jeremy leans me on the forehead and then attempts to kiss me on the lips. I push him away and head towards the bedroom to see if I can see signs a bitch been in my room.

"I don't know why you go in there looking for something your tripping Parker!"

I ignored his antics and began grabbing his clothes out of my closet and packing them in a red Nike duffel bag. I then headed to the bathroom where I went to grab all of his hygiene products out of my house. When I opened the medicine cabinet, I saw a note that read.

Nice Place ...

-xoxo Taylor

He had this bitch in my house. Before I could even confront him, I hear a loud commotion in the living room. I hurry towards the sound to see what was going on.

"Fuck you, bro, I'm not scared of you!" Nose leaking and eyes swelling up by the second.

"You think you about to disrespect my sister and her house nigga I'll kill yo ass."

My brother had beat the dog shit out of Jeremy. I ran over to Keith, begging him not to hit Jeremy anymore.

I was standing in there in between two men whom I loved to the ends of the earth. I cried and yelled for Jeremy to get his things and leave before things got worst.

"Go! Just go, Mac, you don't love me. Just leave!"

He angrily hobbled to the room and grabbed as much stuff as he could hold and walked stormed out of the house.

"You go to Keith!" He was shocked at me telling him to leave my house.

"I asked you to let me handle it, and you didn't have to hit him like that!"

Keith took a step back and gave me a look of hurt and rage.

"That nigga disrespecting my sister and you don't want me to do nothing?! My sister, it's my job to protect you!"

He was right, and he did what any brother would do. It was just that, I loved Jeremy, and I didn't want it to end the way that it did.

"Your right," I said broken-heartedly as I curled up on the couch and whaled out all of the pain and embarrassment I felt.

I then felt the soft, gentle touch of my little brother pulling me into his chest for a hug.

"It's okay sis. I got you."

Chapter 15
Carissa Humphrey

Today was the day for my baby shower, and I was far from excited. I was nervous more than anything. My breasts were sore, my back was hurting, and my feet were swollen, but I was still cute. Don't get it twisted.

I'm about eight months pregnant right now and as tired as ever. With all the drama between my family and Niko's family, it was tough to get this baby shower together.

Niko and I found a cute place in Gardena. Since we moved in together officially, he follows me around the house all the time. He says he doesn't want me to lift a finger. I guess most would say it's cute, but to keep it real, he's getting on my damn nerves. He won't even let me breathe alone. That's my baby though I wouldn't want it any other way.

"You ready to head to the venue pooh?"

Makenzie says to me as she does the final adjustments on the back of my baby shower dress ensuring that all my goods sit just right for my pictures. I had no clue what my baby shower theme was or where was it going to be.

My mom and my friends didn't want me to worry about anything regarding my shower and enjoy the day. They didn't have to tell me to relax more than once. When Niko was locked up; I was working harder than any pregnant woman should, ensuring he had everything he needs. When he came home he made me quit my job so I can focus on school and that's it.

He has been super supportive and proved himself to be a provider since he been home. My baby turned our garage into his mini barbershop and has even enrolled himself in a barber school. Don't get me wrong; there are days they this fool be out with Carter all night doing who knows what, but he told me to trust his process, so I'm just gone shut the hell up and let him show me something.

"You look bomb as hell girl, this baby shower about to break the internet." Makenzie was in charge of getting me and Niko to the shower.

We don't know whether we are having a boy or a girl. The only people that know are Kiani, Makenzie, Miranda, and my momma. We told them the names we have for the baby for a boy or a girl so when we walk into the shower the name is supposed to be somewhere big so we can know what we are having.

If we have a boy, he is going to be a junior, Niko Cameron Grant by Niko's request. If it's a girl her name is going to be Noelle Camille Grant. I want a healthy baby at the end of it all. This was a hard pregnancy dealing with the beginning of it not having my partner with me. I don't know how women raise kids alone. I didn't think I could even continue this pregnancy without him.

"Alright, I'm ready to go who driving?"

I ask as I do my final spin in the mirror checking myself out.

"You and Niko gone ride together I'm gonna drive separate so it can be an extra car to bring gifts back." Makenzie was in charge of making sure we left the house at a particular time, I wonder what the hell these people got planned.

We head out in Niko's Jeep Wrangler, and it's so hard for me to climb in that car. Lately, he has to give me a push up into the car by my bottom.

" You know what, Rissa?"

"What's up, baby?" I look over at him as I buckle my seat belt.

"I couldn't imagine being at this point in my life without you. It's because of you that I see greater for myself. I'm so proud to say that you are carrying my baby." It was moments like this that I knew everything that I been through with Niko was worth it.

He may have seemed like a lost cause to my brother and others, but what he's now realizing in himself, I saw the whole time. Seeing the growth of a man from hanging out on the corners to working, providing and educating himself it was a beautiful transition to witness, and I wish this transition of progression for every black man struggling to get out of his circumstances.

We arrive at the venue address, and we were at the Maria boat docks. We find a parking spot and sight

Kiani in the parking lot walking towards our car with a radio in her hand.

"They arrived; everyone gets in place... hey y'all! Come on, we gotta get you to the boat" Kiani waves us down.

Niko came on my side of the car and grabbed me, placing me down on the ground so I won't have to make a big step from the jeep. His strong arms felt so perfect, gripping my body. He smelled so good wearing that new cologne I got him. My man looked like a straight snack today if I wasn't already pregnant, with him looking and smelling like this I was gone get pregnant today. He had on a black Valentino button-down top with a colorful firework print, some destroyed denim black jeans and some black Mason Margiela sneaker. He set it off with a gold Cuban link chain and a diamond bezel gold Rolex watch.

He wasn't the only one looking good now. Don't get it twisted. My hair was slaying in a slick high ponytail with a natural dewy makeup look with a nude gloss. I was wearing a gold beaded mermaid style dress with some gold Tory Burch sandals because my feet were too swollen for my heels I bought for this dress.

We walked hand and hand towards the exact boat following a few steps behind Kiani.

"Y'all are going to love it! I'm so excited for y'all to see!" Kiani says as she points to the exact boat of the shower making sure to radio in to let the others know we arrived.

When we walked onto the main deck of the boat, blue confetti and balloons fell onto Niko and I from the doorway.

"It's a boy!"

Everyone rejoiced as Niko grabbed me, giving me a big bear hug.

"I love you, Carissa; you gave me a real family," he whispered in my ear before we shared an intimate kiss as if nobody was in the room.

We heard the cooing and cheers from the crowd but at that moment, it was just Niko, Junior, and I.

"Get a picture on my phone!" I hear Miranda say as she wipes her tears. She was a sucker for love just like me.

As we walk through the main deck of the boat, it's Adorned with royal blue and gold balloons with white roses. As we get towards the treats table, I notice that that base of it spells out JUNIOR in all capital letters covered in white and gold roses.

The table was covered with every sweet treat imaginable in dipped in blue and white chocolate with gold trimming. On the left, there was an ice sculpture on the table that said JR and on the right end, there were are maternity pictures on the beach.

This day couldn't have been more perfect. Everyone surrounded us with love and warm wishes, but I could tell something was missing for Niko.

"What's wrong Niko are you okay?"

"I'm okay baby, I mean I ... I don't know where my momma and sister are at, and why they not here."

We knew the baby shower was coming, and with the fight between Kiani and Nakea, my request was for Kiani not to do any retaliation at the baby shower. She agreed, and since she planned the baby shower, her scary ass hired off duty police officers to act as security for the boat.

His family invitations were sent off when everyone else's was. They decided not to show up today. I was told that the invitations stated a strict arrival time by my mom. I want him to feel as happy, and as included in this day as I do so I give him a big hug and love him the way I know-how.

"Let's call her before the boat leaves the dock to see how far she is baby."

"Yeah ... yeah, let's do that cause it's fucked up man why she not here."

She got my baby in his feelings hard right now. I hope she answers this damn phone too.

He and I walked over to the outside deck to make the call without any distractions.

"Aye ma! Where y'all at man?!" Niko says looking hopeful that she says she is walking through the door.

I hear her on the other end of the phone, yelling at the people in traffic.

"Baby! I'm trying to get there. This damn traffic is no joke. Why would y'all have some shit this far anyway." Ms. Keisha wasn't one to get out of the house or from around her neighborhood too often.

"Hey, mommy! The boat is about to take off in a minute. Are you ready to turn up?!" Kiani steps out peeks out on the putter deck to hype me up.

"Girl, we gotta wait for Keisha and them, tell the man to wait before he take-off please."

Her eyes got big, and in panic, she radios out to for someone to tell the captain to wait.

Before she can make to the lower deck to inform the staff, we are waiting for other people before we set sail the boat was already taking off.

Fuck my life right now.

"Man ma the boat is taking off! Y'all knew what time this shit started man." Niko was livid.

"Aye tell them to stop this fucking boat blood!" Everybody with a radio was scrambling to talk to who was in charge of the sail time. In moments a staff member came on the outer deck to let us know that once the boat takes off if it is required to go back they will not set sail again.

"Man I don't care about that shit just go back my mom is in the parking lot." Niko's face planted on the phone rushing his family to get to the dock.

Once we made it back to the dock and his family arrived on the boat, the whole vibe changed. Kiani and Carter were uncomfortable due to their drama with Nakea. And Ms.Keisha wouldn't say one word to me.

You can't take niggas anywhere lovely, and my baby shower made it evident. Throughout the party, I kept seeing the servers rush to replenish the food, which was self serve for the guest. I knew that the caterer was supposed to be bomb, but I didn't know it was going to be gone so quickly.

When I did my rounds to each person's table to guess the inches around the stomach, I was able to get a good look at the culprits? Of course, its Ms. Keisha, Nakea, and their family with to-go plates piled up and even some bagged up under the seat.

"Do you want to measure my tummy for the game?" I ask, generally to their table.

Nakea dryly responded. "Naw, I don't play baby shower games." Followed by looking over at her mother who acted as though I didn't just say anything at all.

"We good, thank you."

I always knew they didn't care for me too much, but today, they have shown their ass.

Niko steps in the center of the main room to give a toast as I sit off to the side, admiring his growth.

"Alright man, y'all know I'm not the best nigga with my emotions and shit. But umm. I just wanted to make a toast to Carissa to show my appreciation."

My baby, one to be much of a talker but when he spoke people gravitated to him. Everyone in the baby shower had the attention of Niko whether they were recording him on their phone or watching the speech at the moment.

Niko turned to me and spoke as if it was just us in the room.

"I want you to know how much I love you. A nigga ain't ever been exposed to so much positive shit until I met you. You believed in me so much that I finally start believing in myself. I thank you for carrying my seed and giving me a family."

Emotions ran high in the room as Niko grabbed me out of the chair and wrapped his arms around me to share a dance on the floor.

"You gonna be my wifey soon, baby. I love you."

Everyone rejoiced and cheered as I rocked in his arms to our jam Before I Let Go by Frankie Beverly and Maze.

More people hopped on the dance floor, and before you know it, we had a whole soul train line going up on the boat.

After a while, I had to sit my ass down and my ole shadow Niko was right beside me, and I guess the photographer thought it was the perfect time for all the group pictures. My girls circled us acting up in the photos along with Niko's friends and some close clients.

"Okay, I want both families in a group photo." The photographer says as the family huddles around us. Ms.Kiesha came on and stood beside me and whispered in my ear.

"You can't keep my son away from me little bitch." Loud enough for only me to hear.

I couldn't believe it. I don't know what I did for her not like me so much. It's so emotionally draining dealing with his family.

I tried to keep a smile for the camera, but the tears just began to fall.

"Wait, what's wrong, baby? You hurting somewhere." As soon as Niko glanced over at me and saw me crying, everything and everyone stopped.

"I just don't know if I can handle it, baby." The tears began to fall uncontrollably, and I began to sob.

Niko pulled me to the side, and my mom and Kiani followed behind.

"What happened?" My mom stood on my side, rubbing my back.

"Niko... baby your .. your mom whispered in my ear and called me a ... a bitch when we were taking the picture." Stuttering and sniffling between my words.

Niko has a confused and defeated look on his face, while my momma had a look of rage. Kiani stood there with one leg shaking trying to make true to her promise of not acting a fool at my shower.

"Hell Naw I know she not calling my baby a got damn thang... Kiesha! Kiesha can you come here please?" My mom was fed up with Niko's whole family.

Ms. Kiesha walked over with a cold look on her face like she was ready to go to war with my mother.

"Aye ma, you called my girl a bitch? Why would you do that?" Niko asked with a look on his face of hope that she didn't say it.

"I sure did, what I said was she not gone keep my son away from me." Standing firm on her statement as if I was the enemy.

"Girl you not gone disrespect, my daughter, I didn't raise her to disrespect her elders. But you can holler at me if you want to Kiesha what's good .. bitch!"

"Come on then Carla ain't nobody scared you planned this whole baby shower and didn't even include his fucking mother fuck you too!"

Niko looked overwhelmed as he tried to keep our mothers from knocking each other's heads off.

Everything around me was turning into a fucking circus. I sat there in disappointment and despair at the mess these people have made of my baby shower.

When I got up to try to get their attention and get them to stop arguing, I felt a stream of water come down my leg to my feet.

I was completely stuck as I attempt to look down at my feet and see what was going on. That's when Kiani noticed and rushed to my side to make me sit back down.

"Niko! Niko! Her water broke, we gotta get her to the hospital!"

Niko turned towards me, shocked with a scared look on his face.

"You okay baby? Aye somebody help me get her shit to the car man." He grabbed me in one swoop and carried me off the boat and to the car.

Our mothers run behind following bickering on whose fault it is that my water broke early.

Niko sat me in the car put strapped me in the seat belt, slammed the door and turned to our mommas standing outside the door.

"Look, this shit is too much for my girl and if y'all can't get this shit together y'all ain't gotta be around." My mom was furious, and she couldn't believe that he was trying to check them like that.

"Who the fuck are you talking to? You need to talk to yo momma talking to my baby crazy!"

This shit was getting nowhere fast, so I just screamed Niko's name to get his attention.

He turned towards my window and assured me that we were headed to the hospital.

"We can all for sure talk another day, but if you can't act right don't follow us to no hospital."

Niko hopped on the car, kissed me on the cheek, and we rushed out of the parking lot and headed to the hospital.

"No matter what Carissa, we family. Fuck what my momma was talking about." Niko said as we pulled up the Dock Emergency Care Hospital parking lot.

Chapter 16
Jeremy McCall

"Why you always lien about what you are doing, Mac?" Taylor says as she packs the delivery bag for the hospital.

"Tay, man nobody, is lien I love you man, I got friends, but I don't want nobody as I want you."

This pregnancy shit has been a complete turn off for me. I'm not ready for a fucking baby. I thought I was, but in actuality, I'm still trying to be young and live my life.

"You're so selfish, you only think about yourself. I thought this baby would make you a little more considerate of how you make people feel but your freaking worst."

185

I'm fed up my nigga. She doesn't think about me. I want to be able to provide completely for my kid. I mean I told her I want her to have my baby but damn, not now.

"Man what made you think now is the right time to have a baby ?! Does it look like I'm ready? No, I'm still in school Tay."

She stopped what she was doing, turned to me tears streaming down her rosy cheeks.

"I can't make you be ready Mac, so get out. You don't have to be here... I'll do this shit by myself."

I've never seen this side of Taylor before. She is usually down to go back and forth with me in a heated argument or something petty. She knows that I love her, and in the future, she is who I want to commit myself to entirely. But why she gotta put this baby on me right now I got enough stress.

She knows my mom has been sick and in ICU for the past couple of months and my Pops is on the other side of the country. I don't have any family, no help. I'm doing this shit out here on my own doing what I gotta do to survive, and she wants to bring a baby in the picture. I don't think I can handle it.

"Man Tay you gonna kick me out? After all these years you turning your back on me?"

She turned to me with a look of disgust like I made her sick to her stomach.

"Yeah, get out of my tranquil space." As she got up to burn sage around the room. "You think I don't know you had me at some girl house the other day? By the way ... your eye is looking a little puffy she must have seen that note I left in the bathroom." Casually, as she sat down and continued to sort out the baby clothes.

"You did what? How dare you ruin my relationships with people like that? Fuck you! I don't need this shit I got enough shit going on right now." I grabbed my shit and dashed out of her house, headed towards the bus stop.

"I don't know what is wrong with these women, nowadays they think they can go and do catty shit to one another to keep me from having other female company, they're sick!"

On days like these, when these females try to stress me out, its an excellent time to see my moms.

I take the 51 down to City Beach Hospital to check on my mom. Usually, Taylor checks in on her every day when she is at work. But since she is on pregnancy leave, my momma has not had any visitors.

I know I sound like a terrible son, but y'all don't understand. It's hard seeing your mom lay in that hospital and you scared for her fate daily. I can't deal with it, especially because I gotta do what I need to do to survive right now a nigga been out here feeling like an orphan.

Once I made it to the ICU floor, I start to feel nauseous. As you walk past each glass room you can see people laying with tubes and machines everyone in a place seems like will be their final destination.

I make it to my mother's room, and I see her lay there fast asleep.

"Ma, mommy I'm here, can you hear me?" I say softly in her ear as I caress her cold hands.

"Hello sweetie, we had to put your mother in a state of sedation to allow her body to rest, her heart rate was going up to high." A nurse walks in and tells me in hopes that I wouldn't keep trying to wake her up.

"Wait for what? How long do you guys plan to have her in this state? What's wrong with her heart ?"

The nurse looked overwhelmed with the questions and gave me the same tired ass line they give when they want you to go home.

"Her body was working too hard when she was awake, and she needs to rest. I will have the doctor call your phone Jeremy, why don't you try to go get some rest."

They always trying to get somebody to go home. I'm barely here anyway, and I'm still getting encouraged to leave.

With a feeling of defeat, I kiss my sedated mother on the forehead and head out of the hospital feeling worse than when I came.

I sit in the main lobby of the hospital, overnight bag in hand to figure out my next move for tonight, and I need a drink or some white get my mind together.

Shit, all this I'm going through with Tay and Parker, I could've stayed fucking with Makenzie and her running all my bitches away.

I bite my pride and give go through my contacts to give her a call. The phone rings a couple of times and then went to voice mail.

"Oh she trying to act like she still mad, she knows she can't get enough of me."

I send her a text message letting her know that I missed her and wanted to talk. To my surprise o get an immediate response.

MAKENZIE: My man wouldn t appreciate you texting or calling my phone.

What? She got a nigga now. I just had to laugh. She had to go pick up some dude out of the woodworks to try to get over me huh? That's hilarious. It's alright I know I'll get her.

Bzzzz

My phone rings suddenly and it's my boy AJ.

"What's the deal bro pull up we about to have a function at my house." Ah just what I needed.

"Alright bet I'm on my way!"

❧

I made it to AJ's house bottle in my bag, ready to turn up.

As I'm walking up to the house, I noticed a familiar car parked on the street. What was Parker doing at AJ house without me this was my brother.

I knock on the door, and the house was clouded with smoke. The house was so smoky you could get high off contact. The music was bumping so hard you can feel the bass in your body. This was my kinda party. First thing first, I was going to walk the house to see where the fuck Parker was at.

"What's the deal bro, roll up!" AJ brings me in for a handshake and hugs with the blunt in one hand.

"What's the deal bro, I got the weed nigga. I got some drink where the bitchesss at?" I say jokingly as I head towards the bedroom to sit my bag.

Once I come out of the bedroom, I get a good look at everyone in the living room. I don't see Parker, but I know I see her car outside. Fuck it whatever; it's other females in here to talk to anyway.

"Hey, Mac baby what's good." I heard Karly say as she sat next to me on the living room couch. She didn't sit next to me on the couch though; she was all over nigga legs propped up on my thigh, and she acting like she wanted to fuck with me right in the middle of the function. She was bad, deep chocolate complexion in some high rise jeans showing her coke bottle figure and a yellow crocheted half-shirt no bra so you can see the nipple rings peeking through the top.

The partying was going, and females were everywhere dancing. Shaking ass, drinking, just having a good time. I was drunk as fuck, trying to forget about the long day I had between baby momma drama and visiting my momma.

Suddenly, a new crowd of girls walked into the house, and that's when I saw Parker's little frame sashay through the house towards the kitchen. My alcohol is getting the best of me, so I head towards the kitchen to where she was. Grin on my face, I walk around and speak to all the homegirls from school except her.

She looked me up and down as if she was waiting for me to attempt to speak to her. Fuck that I wasn't saying shit, the key to the game is to treat them like they did something to you.

"That will get her attention."

I headed back to the living room and put Karly on my lap, and we talked for the rest of the night until the party slowed down, and I walked her out to her car. When ahead back towards the house, little Parker meets me at the front door and comes marching up to me in rage.

"So you just gonna talk to someone new in my face?" I told y'all these bitches like drama. If you wanna get their attention and they not speaking to you bag a badder bitch in their face. They gonna be sick.

Parker wasn't the best looking chick, but she was cute to me. She was short as fuck stopping only at my chest and a cool 4'11. Big ass titties I'm surprised her little body can hold them up. She had a big ass head too but my baby was cool that was my dawg she always looked out for me.

"You ain't said shit to me all night now you wanna press me about who I talk to? Ha Taylor, please."

She looked at my nose, turned and forehead wrinkled like she was a bull ready to charge.

"So you calling me Taylor now? That's the game you play? For sure fuck you!" Her voice cracking as she screamed I fucked up. I know I'm playing a game, but I didn't mean to call her Taylor for real. These women got me stressed out. I grabbed Parker by the arm and engulfed her into my chest with a huge hug not letting her go.

"I'm so sorry baby I love you, I fucked up okay?" I whisper in her ears while kissing her on her forehead.

"Move Jeremy, and I hate you. You always hurt me." She replies in a tearful defeated tone.

"I know I fucked up, I know. I love you though Parker please ride with me," I pleaded.

She nodded her head, looked up at me with here eye ducks full of tears.

"I love you, Mac, stop hurting me please."

"I got you a MiniP. I got you."

Chapter 17
Makenzie Gray

My voice echoed through the room as I moaned out at the strokes of Palms Springs bae.

"Yaaas daddy don't stop" I yelled as I push my hips back to meet his stroke.

"Uhhh, huh, you like that?" followed by a hard smack on my ass stinging my left cheek.

We bumped and grind until we both collapsed face forward into the bed. Shit has been going great between Rick and me, yeah that's his name. He was everything I was trying to pry out of Jeremy, but I didn't have to pull it out of him. It was like as soon as I acknowledged my prideful ways in Palms Springs, God gave me an immediate blessing with brining this amazing man into my life. I prob shouldn't be having premarital sex huh? You know what, God knows my heart.

"You got some good pussy girl, you about to have me tripping out here," Rick says in a joking manner.

Things have been going good between us, dating him has opened my eyes to so many things a man does for his woman that I'm so used to doing myself.

In high school, I took auto- mechanics class so I could know how to change my oil and fix my tires when need be, I didn't need to ask any nigga for no help. Welp, my independence was shut the fuck down just recently by Rick. The other day we were leaving from the Grove from seeing a movie and my tire popped while exiting the parking lot. I immediately went into mechanic bae mode pulling over and getting my jack to lift my car out the trunk without even saying a word to him. Rick hopped out the car once he realized what I was doing and stared at me in amazement that I was willing to get my acrylics dirty.

"Bae, get yo sexy ass off the floor fucking with this car, I didn't even know you were over here doing this shit. Let me take care of you girl damn!"

He put his hand out to help me up off the ground and politely opened the driver door for me to sit my ass down. After he finished changing the tire he sat back in my passenger seat and looked over me dumbfounded.

"What makes you think I'm going to let you struggle in my presence?" I didn't know what to say. I never thought of it as a way of struggling. I do what I gotta do, and I have to be able to make sure I'm straight man of no man.

"I didn't think about it as struggling" while shrugging my shoulders and pulling my hair behind my ears. " Its second nature for me just to get things done for me," I said adjusting my seatbelt before pulling off. Before I could put the car in drive he touched my arm to get my full attention and said to me in a stern tone.

"Your my girl now you ain't gotta do all that shit no more. I'm right here."

I'd be lien if I didn't say that it was hard for me to believe the shit he was saying . I'm a little tougher than most, and I battle with it constantly. It's hard maintaining your femininity when you know you can't depend on a nigga for shit.

But that wasn't my story anymore, and I had a man that was trying to love me and I was making it hard for him to do so. I had some serious work to do, I thought to myself as we headed back to his apartment.

After a couple more rounds of passion. I get up shower and cook some chicken tacos, rice, and black beans. I head back to the room to wake him up for dinner.

"Damn, how long was I sleep you cooked all this?" while grabbing his plate and headed towards the couch to turn on the tv.

"No no no, we are sitting at the table tonight, let's talk," I say while waving towards the dining table.

"What you wanna talk about the girl? You already done had me sleep have my day away off that pussy, I can't watch sports either?" He rolled his eyes and headed towards the dining table. Once he sat down he shook his head at me impatiently like he was waiting to see something spectacular happen.

"Don't rush me liked that, Ricky!" I yelp playfully, as I sat down at the table.

"I just wanted to let you know that I appreciate you ... that's all" guilty look on my face because I know damn well that ain't all I wanted to say. This opening up is hard to do.

"Man you had me turn off sports center to say that?" Grabbing at his gold Cuban link chain, adjusting his charm.

"No, I just know I been making it hard for you lately and I want you to know I do appreciate you and I'm trying."

With a smirk on his face, he takes a bite out of his taco.

"Trying to what Makenzie?"

"I'm trying to .. I don't know exactly, be needier I guess." With a shrug of my shoulders, I continued to eat my food.

"You ain't gotta be needy, and I know you stubborn my nigga. But all that strong shit you have been on is going out the window anyway. You sprung baby girl." This boy lost his mind. I rolled my eyes and continued to eat when my phone rang.

I look at the name that pops up, and it's Jeremy. Glancing up at Rick I show him the phone.

"Pick that muthafucka up, and tell cuh to stop calling you." Don't get me wrong, that's what I wanted to do anyway, but when a nigga put the pressure on you, you get a little nervous.

I was hesitant to answer the phone initially, but I picked up and put it on speaker.

"Hello?" I said in a confused tone.

"Hello, Kenz?! Baby where you at I need you right now please." He sounded like he was crying, the sound of him breaking down broke my heart internally, but I had to put on a strong front.

" Jeremy, please stop calling me, I already told you I got a nigga now." I hang up the phone and continue to eat my food.

"That nigga gonna call again when he does let me pick up the phone." This is too much I don't want to deal with the drama.

Sure enough, Jeremy called again and before I could even blink Rick had the phone in his hand and headed to the room. I tried to follow behind, but Rick gave me a deathly stare and told me to go sit down and closed the room door. I went and sat my ass down, but tiptoed back to listen at the door. I couldn't hear a muthafucking thing. Suddenly I heard the clocking back of a gun and a pound on the door. I quickly ran back to the couch to appear to look like I never got up.

Shortly after Rick came back into the living room with my phone in hand and threw it on the couch.

"I want a fucking block on the phone Yvette!" He yells with a chuckle.

"I'm just playing cuh, but he ain't gone call no more that's over with." I looked at Rick intrigued by his recent actions behind that door.

"What did you say, Ricky?" I asked coming in to wrap my arms around him for a hug.

"Man, don't worry about it; some shit women don't need to worry about. Just know it's over with."

Chapter 18
Miranda Beal

I'm sick and tired of this bitch. She really needs to get out of my house.

"I know you got something going on with Taylor Judith; you think somebody is dumb or something?." I yell from the kitchen slamming pots and pans around in the sink as I clean.

"Miranda you need to stop tripping for real nothing is going on I got you I'm good!" Walking towards me in the kitchen trying to reach in for a kiss.

"No get off of me for real I don't want to be bothered no more. All you do is sit yo ass around here while I do everything. How am I suppose to be with somebody who can't teach me shit?"

Her face began to redden as she stopped in her tracks, shocked at what I had said.

"Oh, for real Miranda I cant teach you shit? You think I'm a charity case or something, my nigga?!" If we were being honest, yes the fuck I did. She didn't do shit if I didn't hold her hand step by step, the only reason she got the job she has now is because I take her to work every day and I applied for that shit for her.

"Girl just get the hell out my house I'm tired of being your baby sitter." As I waved her out of my way while I headed to the restroom. She followed behind, but I slammed the door shut, locking her out.

"You walk around her trying to act all prim and proper, as you fucking better than me and now I'm a child? I don't need you to babysit me I'm grown! Fuck you, Miranda!"

All she was saying was going through one ear and out of the other as I turn on the shower to prepare for my night of passion.

I was tired of Judith, and I think it was time for me to let my bob down and live life.

A couple of weeks ago, I had run into the white boy who lived in the basketball house where Makenzie had that fight. I knew who he was instantly, but I played cool and acted like I didn't see him. We were in the student union, and I was sitting at the Coffee Cafe when he spotted me.

"Aye... aye where I know you from ma?" He stood about 6'7 pale white skin covered in a collage of tattoos from the neck down. Light brown eyes, full lips with a cute smile bright smile that gleamed in the sun. Clean cut in the face with a neatly lined up beard. He rocked a comb-over hair cut with a part on the side and was wearing our school's basketball gear.

"You may have seen me at a school event," I respond dryly returning my attention to my laptop and trying not to show my interest in such a guy.

He invited himself to sit down with me and stared me down until I redirected my attention from my computer screen to him.

"May I help you ?" I ask readjusting my glasses on my face and putting one side of my red bob behind my ear.

"Yo, don't do that ma! I wanna figure out where I saw you at.... aye I remember you one of the girls that ran in my house starting a fight."

My face flustered with embarrassed I immediately responded.

"I don't recall." And put my face back into my computer screen Aimlessly browsing the internet.

He reaches out across the table and closes my laptop.

"Dead ass, has anybody told you how rude it is not to acknowledge when someone is talking to you shorty?" I looked at him in shock, I know damn well he didn't just close up my computer.

"I'm trying to study and you're being a distraction," I respond saying. He chuckled at my cool demeanor like he knew it was a front.

"Stop playing and give me your number ma, you owe me that much all the shit you started that night at my house." I figured fuck it, why not give him the number. I don't have to reply.

"Sure, it's 281-330-8004," I said as he put the number on his phone.

He looked up and looked sideways at me, and we both busted up laughing.

"Aye shorty stop playing, you know what give me your phone I know how to get you."

He took my phone off the table and put his number in followed by calling himself to ensure he had my number too.

"I'm going to call you tonight around 8 o'clock when I leave practice so make sure your free."

"Okay," I say looking dumbfounded that I let this white boy run game on me like this.

"I'm Liam, but everyone calls me LB and what's your name?" Reaching out, grabbing my hand.

"I'm Miranda." As I stared and admired the tattoos up his arm.

Liam knew he had my attention.

"Next time you come over my house, it's going to be a real invitation, and not you busting in."

He says before getting up and going on his way.

That was our first encounter, and we have been texting and chatting and hanging out at his place every since. The more I have been talking to him the more I realize how tired of Judith I am. I want to be around someone that I feel can teach me something. I want some growth in my life, and I was tired of her immaturity.

She bangs on the bathroom door.

"Miranda, you about to hop in the shower like we not talking?" I ignore her and shoot a text to Liam to let him know what time to come over for dinner tonight. This was going to be his first time coming to my place since I have a squatter living here. I was so excited about finally living life.

"Fuck it then I'll leave, your right I have been fucking with Taylor!" She wanted me to come out of the bathroom and knock her out. But I am in a different place and I really don't give a damn what she does as long as she gets out of my house.

I turn on my Bluetooth speaker blast my music and hop in the shower.

♫ See I'm just about over being your girlfriend
(I'm leaving)
I'm leaving
No more wondering what you been doing where you been sleeping
(It's over)
I'm leaving♫

BOOM BOOM

"So, you gonna play some fucking Chrisette Michelle like I ain't shit bitch?... fuck you Miranda."

I hear some banging in the room and then a final bang at the front door.

"Finally, I can't enjoy my space!" I yelp as I finish washing up in the shower. I head towards the room, and I see clothes all over the floor and drawers hanging out of the dresser for me to clean.

"This is why I'm done with yo ass too can't ever clean up shit."

In my powder pink silky robe, I cleaned up my mess of a room and started dinner.

I made Italian sausage and spinach lasagna with a garden salad and garlic knots. I tried to make my little circle dining table look exciting by putting a silver bucket in the middle with ice and red wine.

I tidied up in the kitchen and lit my candles all around the house. With this being his first time chilling at my place I wanted it to be more romantic. I went inside my bedroom and did a quick natural beat to my face with some lashes and a nude lipgloss that appeared to be a warm brown against my vanilla complexion.

I went into the closet to look to see what I was going to wear for our special night and I hear a knocking on the door.

"I told this girl to leave my house. I know her ass not coming back." I marched off to the front door in my silky robe and underwear ready to go off. When I swung open the door there was Liam.

"Damn ma, this how you open the door for people?" As he welcomed himself into my house and sat on the couch like he owned the place.

"It smells good as fuck in here yo! Dead ass, you don't know what you asking for ma."

I gave him a smirk and excused myself to my room to put on a quick tie-dye sundress and pink fuzzy Ugg house slippers.

"Well, hello, welcome to my place!" I say to him while heading to the kitchen.

"We have been in your domain every time we hang out it's about time you are welcomed into my place."

I make our plates and place them on the dining table, and wave for him to have a seat.

Dinner was every bit of fantastic we laughed and joked and talked about our goals after college and onward. In my meeting him I had a different idea of the type of guy he would be. I felt like he was just another culture vulture white boy trying to fit in. But in getting to know him I learned a lot about his history and how he grew up in the Bronx raised by his black foster mom and all his siblings he had growing up was black. So while most people assume he is acting and trying to be something he is not. He is just being the only person he knows how to be.

"Yo, real shit. I ain't never had a girl cook no fire ass meal for me like that ever." He says while wiping his mouth and staring at me like I was the final course.

"You trying to get me to wife you up or what? Cause dead ass that's what it's looking like." I smiled at the thought of dating him. But to be real, I was scared as hell. I haven't had a boyfriend since my freshman year of high school. I don't know the first thing about building or getting close to a guy. But I most definitely wanted to know what the workings of males anatomy were all about.

"Oh, hush LB you don't know what to do with a gal like myself," I say playfully while walking around the back of his chair and hugging him around his neck.

He swiftly brought me around to his lap and kissed me passionately wrapping his arms around my waist and then gripping my thighs.

"Soooo... what's for dessert?" He says biting his bottom lip. Unexpectedly, he picks me up and carries me to my room.

He laid me down gently on my bed and began pulling my panties to the side and feasting on my lady parts. I found myself lost in the pleasure of his touch and his kisses. Things were heating up fast, and I found myself not knowing what to do next. I don't know the first thing about being with a guy.

He could sense the nerves in my face and ask me was I okay. I nodded yes and brought his face to mine for a passionate kiss. I was as ready as I was going to be. He pulled a gold wrapper out of his pocket and slid his jimmy on smoothly. He looked me in my eyes, and as he inserted himself he went in for another kiss exhaling with each stroke. I gotta say, this seems like something I could get used to.

We bumped and grind the remainder of the night until we went fast asleep. A loud slam of the front door woke us up as I heard Judith come in still on bull shit.

"Miranda I'm coming for the rest of my shit, and I'm sleeping on the couch tonight. You got me fucked up if you think you about to kick me out of OUR shit like I don't pay rent in this muthafucka!" Before I could say a word here come Judith busting in the bedroom door.

"What the fuck, oh that's what you are doing for real? After everything you gone go get with some fucking white boy?" She says while pulling up her basketball shorts like she was getting ready to square up.

"You fucking rat on everything I love bruh." She charged at me, but before she could lay a finger, Liam intervened.

"Yo ma chill out with all that shit, she doesn't want you anymore, take it to try chin and bounce." Pointing back at the front door.

"What the fuck? Who are you, my nigga!? You gone let this muthafucka tell me to get out ?!" Yelling at me on the other side of Liam's arm.

"Bitch fuck you! I hope this nigga fuck you over and that's on my momma!" Pounding her chest you can hear the crackle in her voice as tears streamed down her face.

I was truly tired of Judith, and I honestly didn't give a damn about her hurting. I was hurting from all the stupid, unreliable shit she has done. Rent being late, quitting jobs like she doesn't have responsibilities. She was fucking around with bitches from her jobs. I politely waved goodbye to her as she stormed out of the apartment slamming the door.

"So that's her, huh?" Liam said, coming back from locking the door.

"Yeah, that's her," I say with a roll of my eyes not wanting to further a conversation about me and her's relationship.

"Yo Ma, Idk how y'all shit is in Cali, but if a chick catches me with someone new in our crib she ain't just leaving and not coming back. We need to head to my place for the night."

I guess he had a point, JuJu is crazy, and she looks like she was ready to knock my ass out.

"Alright let me pack a bag real quick so we can head out," I say as I get up and head towards the closet.

"Yo, get some shit for the week dead ass I don't trust that shit. Ain't nobody gone be hurting my shorty."

I walked out of some bullshit to walk right into something that seemed like a better fit. Was I moving to fast? Maybe, but it was time for little miss reserved Miranda to let her hair down and live for herself.

.

Chapter 19
Niko Grant

"Aye nigga, what're the moves for tonight bro!" Carter asks as we smash down the 110 headed to Hollywood.

It was my nigga bachelor party, and I had to do it big for em. We had the whole function already going just waiting for us to arrive. It was Carter, Rick and I in my jeep headed to the Hollywood Hills.

Shit with our families has been crazy and tonight was gone be the night to get the fuck away from all the bull shit. Carissa had my little nigga Jr, and he is as perfect as ever. My momma pulled some weak shit at the hospital asking the doctor about getting a DNA test in front of my girl. But I didn't go for that shit. I told them if they couldn't be cool they had to leave and surprisingly her, and my sister shut their ass up.

But of course, some messy shit had to come up. In the hospital, Carissa gets pictures posted by Faith sent to her phone with her legs kicked up in my back seat from when I gave her that ride from the strip club. The bitch gone have the nerve to put in the caption. "I'll always have his back - Mrs.Meech." I didn't hear the end of that shit damn near got kicked out of my house. My nigga Cavi had to give alibi on what happened that night leaving the strip club.

I tried to be nice about not fucking with Faith, but she didn't get it. So I had to get the little homegirls to send her a little message.

My sister has been stressing my nigga out playing games with CJ so when I got em I shoot him to Cavi, that way he can see his son. Shit even Rick had to send a little message to that nigga at that school trying to get back with Makenzie. My nigga said the last time the nigga called her he cocked the pistol and told that nigga if he calls his bitch again it was gone be lights out.

So if you don't get it by now, niggas been going through shit too.

Tonight was our night to let go of the goofy shit and turn the fuck up.

"Aye nigga pass the blunt cuhz.. stop babysitting the weed!" Carter yells to the back seat at Rick.

"Nigga shut up! I'm about to roll up another one right now." Rick said. That nigga was known for hogging the blunts, I hate smoking with this foo.

"Nigga, you faced that whole blunt by yo self? This water balloon head nigga selfish foo on the gang" I say as I shake my head refocusing on the road.

"Meechie shut up foo I got pounds back here nigga don't even trip. Y'all niggas face y'all own blunts." Rick says pulling a sack out of his black Fendi backpack.

"That's what the fuck I'm talking about, roll up then nigga," Carter says pulling the tray out of my glove compartment to dump out the backwood.

We finally make it to the house in Hollywood. Niggas were living like Dons renting out fly shit to fuck the city up. The inside of the house was still lit up from the outside, and you can tell shit was already going up. I shoot a text to one of the little homies already in the house to let him know we about to mob in.

Once we walked up, my young nigga open the door and we were welcomed by some thick stripper bitches holding cigar boxes.

Dj Verified was in the house working the tables and welcomed my nigga Cavi to his bachelor party.

"Let's turn it the fuck up for my niggas walking in. My nigga Cavi our here getting married next weekend, Let's get it, Let's go!" As he wiped the sweat from his face with his black rag he always kept in his pocket. My nigga Verified was always sweating bullets since we were kids. The fat nigga couldn't help it I guess.

The view from the house overlooked the city. Niggas felt like they finally made it, parties in glasshouses in the Hills. You really couldn't tell us we wasn't those niggas.

The bachelor party was cracking; strippers were shaking ass everywhere. My nigga Cavi thought he was that nigga with females hanging all over him dancing. The weed was in the air the drank was flowing, and it was just a cool as vibe when we get a banging knock at the door.

"Who the fuck is that blood?" I say as I nod off to Rick to put everyone on alert. We never about to get caught slipping. Rick had on his backpack and is already on the go. I tell the little nigga to open the door and on comes Keith, Faith's little brother. What the fuck did this little nigga want and who even told him about this shit?

"What's up nigga?" I say in a straight demeanor, he always has sneaky ways about him that I didn't rock with.

"What's the deal with y'all and my sister bro?" He says walking up towards me with a cold face.

The strippers began to grab their money and run towards the exit, and some of the Pooh butt ass niggas did too.

"What's up my nigga, you walk up in our shit trying to politic what's cracking!"

Suddenly before me and him could even come to blows two niggas walking in the house charging towards Rick and Carter.

Carter and Rick immediately pull out ready for whatever. Niggas couldn't believe this shit was happening right now especially with this little nigga, but it was no time to reflect on why this was happening. Had to get in action, I socked Keith dead in the nose and watched him collapse. After a scuffle with the other to niggas, I and my homies head out the door hop into my black jeep and dip. I'm guessing Faith knew where that ass whoop'n came from.

I call up my sister and immediately to figure out what the fuck is going on.

"Hello, What you want, fool."

"Aye, who told that little nigga Keith where our shit was gone be at ?"

She was quiet for a second like she knew some shit and didn't wanna tell me.

"What the fuck you been on Nikea?!" Carter yells towards the phone.

There was an awkward silence, and then she burst out in tears.

"I told him where it was going to be, but I just thought he was trying to turn up! I didn't know he was in some revenge shit!" She explained. I know this was my sister but, I wasn't buying this shit she was talking about.

"That was the dumbest shit you could've ever done Nikea almost got us or them niggas fucking popped!"

I hang up the phone with her dumb ass and drive-through Hollywood, trying not to go head directly back home because we may be being followed.

"What we gonna do about this shit foo?"

"We gone have to chip this little nigga or something," Carter says shaking his head in disappointment. This was our little nigga our little runner, and I know this nigga was hot about me getting Faith beat up.

"Fuck that nigga you gonna have to call and give Faith some dick so she can chill out," Rick says in the back seat tucking his gun. This nigga is losing it.

"Nigga I ain't fucking that bitch!" I say immediately he was trying to get me caught up in some shit. Damn, I wish I woulda told that bitch to delete them pictures or I wouldn't have been in this situation right now.

" You gone have to do something nigga, just call her and see what she on."

So many thoughts going through my head, my girl, my family, shit my life being at risk behind this bitch I don't know what to do. I know if I fuck with her I can call all stop and all this shit would be over with. I wouldn't hear a peep from her little peoples no more.

"Hello?" She says on the other end of the phone.

"What you on man? What are you trying to do?" I yell into the phone. Just hearing her voice made me irritated as fuck.

" I don't know what you're talking about nigga; I'm on whatever you on. You send yo people I send mine." She said sounding pretty stern and sure of herself. But I knew how to break that down.

"Be cool bro we need to dead this shit, don't even cuss her out," Carter says reassuring me that calling her was the best thing to do.

"Man I love you Faith, but you already know what the deal is, why you wanna do weak shit when you know the deal?" I figure if I butter her up she will calm it down.

"Why you didn't pick me? I love you Niko! Not her!" Here, she goes with that shit.

"Man where you at? I'm on my way." I tell her driving towards Carter's spot to switch off cars. I leave Rick and Carter at the spot and head over to Faith's house. Some shit I said I'll never do again. But desperate times call for desperate measures and a nigga was desperate.

I pull up to the front of her apartment complex and tell her to come down. Gun in my lap I am not about to get caught slipping fucking with this bitch.

When she came down, she was wearing some little ass spandex shorts and one of her high school cheer t-shirts. She thinks she's about to seduce me, but I got some shit coming for her ass.

"Get out the car Niko come up." She says, standing in the doorway waving for me to come up.

Fuck that if I was gone get popped she getting popped too, we about to be right in this car who knows who she got in that house.

"Naw man come on get in the car." She smiles and then headed towards the silver BMW truck I was driving and hops in. I gotta get her back in the position to do whatever I need her to do. The only way imma be able to do that without the bull shit is to give this bitch what she wants.

"So you wanted to come over here and talk about what Niko?" She says looking at me with a hope that I'll tell her some old romantic fairytale shit. But I just said the magic words that I knew she wanted to hear.

"Man you know what I'm here for, pull him out.

Chapter 20
Carissa Humphrey

The bells the church rang as we processed through the doors to be seated. It seemed like we couldn't catch a fucking break; it just been too much going on. My stomach turned immediately as I caught a glimpse of the white casket set up in front of the pulpit.

"Ahhh nooo I can't do it! I cannot do it y'all!" The mother yelled in agony as her family practically carried her to the church pew. Tears filled my eyes as I held my baby boy and rocked praying that I'll never see the day when I'd have to bury my child.

The pastor said a sermon and the room was filled and all you could hear was the groans of pain from people in each pew. The floral arrangement was white, and powder blue and the projector in the pulpit played a slide show of pictures and memories that we all shared. I don't think the core of the group would ever be the same again after such loss. I know my girl is hurting deeply and I can't imagine her ever being the same.

It was time for people to go up and say some parting words.

"Do you wanna go up and say your poem?" Her mother asked her with tears flowing down her cheeks as if she had lost a child herself.

"I don't think I can do it ma; it's my fault!" She Waled as her mother grabbed her in her arms trying to get her to calm down.

"It's not your fault don't say that imma walk up there with you okay? Everything gonna be okay cause mama is right here."

She agreed and stood up to walk towards the pulpit. Her immediate family all stood up to stand by her side at the pulpit. As soon as it was her turn, she began to renege.

"I can't do it. Please, I don't want to talk." She pleaded with her family.

"It's okay baby. I'll do it for you, and you want me to say your speech for you?" She nodded in reply. As she snuggled under the arms of a family member standing beside her.

" Good evening everyone, I'm going to read this poem on behalf of my child who is not able to do so at the moment." She says to everyone in the crowd.

"You know, this child right here" pointing at the casket " was a second child to me and Deborah if there is anything you need you let me know. I'm going to be over there whatever time of day." She says reassuring the family of the victim of her love for them.

"Okay, now I'm going to go ahead and read this poem written by my daughter to her first love."

"From the moment I saw you, I knew it was a love worth trying. I never knew how much pain I'd feel if I ever lost you. I never imagined a world without you living in it. I'm so sorry I didn't see your pain. I'm sorry I didn't protect you from the shame you felt. You rejoiced with me on my best days and loved me on my worst days. I usually made it a hard thing to love me. I was just afraid, afraid of letting my hair down and being free. No matter how anal or self-righteous I was you made sure to handle me gently and love me the same. I don't know how I could continue living with such pain. Our last words I wish I could take back and hold you one more time. I wish you to come back. I wish I could do it all over again. I wish instead of fighting we could have agreed to be friends. You were my rock when I was alone, and I wish I could tell you to come home... and my daughter Miranda wrote it to her first love, Judith."

A whale of tears began on to come from Miranda as her family carried her off of that pulpit. I was heartbroken for my friend. Her and Judith weren't on the best terms, but she didn't want anything to happen to her. We all been knowing Judith as long as we all have known each other, she was like our sister too.

When Miranda called and told me the news, I had just put my baby to sleep and was up watching my show Paternity Court.

"Rissa !!!!!" I heard her yell on the other side of the phone.

"What's wrong Miranda what happened?" I sit up and head out of the bedroom of my place straight to the bathroom.

"I .. I came back to my apartment after being at Liam's

all week, and Ju Ju was laying in the bathtub dead...
she gone, Rissa!" She yelled through the phone. I didn't
even know what to say or how to comfort her. I just told
her I was on my way.

I was a little nervous about leaving my baby at home
with Niko he is still recovering from his wild weekend
from Carter's bachelor's party. So I called my mommy
to watch Jr and headed to Miranda's. She had already
called the other girls because they were there upon
my arrival.

"I wish I was at home! This would never have happened."
I heard her scream in the street as Makenzie and
Kiana try to console her. Her normally perfect bob was
sweated out and all over here head. Her eyes were
swollen, almost looking shut from the tears. My girl
was looking bad, and I run towards where they were
standing and as soon as she saw me she started to
drop to the floor in agony.

"Why did I leave her! I tried it didn't work! She wouldn't
get it right for me y'all." She was a wreck, pain, sorrow,
and regret filled her body.

"I wish I could take it all back! I wish I could have done
something different!" She screamed.

We took her to her mother's house that night and stayed with her, allowing her to vent and cry in our arms the entire night.

Back at the funeral Taylor, Jeremy's baby mother went up to speak. I look over at Makenzie in the audience as her face struck with envy and hurt at the sight of the girls growing belly. I know my friend carried a lot of regret for not keeping her baby. She felt weak-minded because she let a man push her into doing something she honestly didn't want to do. It was an awkward silence in the room as she unfolded her paper to speak.

There had already been speculation of her and Juju dealings with each other before she passed, which caused the harsh break up between Miranda and Judith.

"This is a poem I wanted to write for my dearest friend and lover." There Gasp from people in the funeral all around. Anyone who knew Judith knew she was with Miranda since forever so when Taylor said that. Minds were wondering.

"I loved you since I laid eyes on you at work. I knew you were the person I was supposed to share my heart and secrets with. I wish this was all a dream and when we decided to be together you would have kept choosing me! I wish you chose me, and you would be right here, I'll love you till the end of the end your Goddaughter will forever know your name. Rest In Peace, my love."

The crowd was in shock, anyone that knew her knew she was with Judith. All you can hear in the funeral was the sounds of Miranda's voice being muffled with her mother's hand.

"Bitch, I knew it... I wish you weren't pregnant I'd beat your.."

"Shhhhh Miranda don't worry about it." Her mother said as she held her baby in her arms. Miranda wept and wept. I've never seen her in so much pain before.

During the funeral, procession Miranda rode in the family car with Judith's mother and her siblings. I couldn't even tell you where Makenzie went she was shaken from seeing a pregnant Taylor and the loss of our JuJu.

After the burial, I drove down the road in the cemetery to visit my father. This is my first time visiting him in a couple of years and figured it would be a good time for him to meet his grandson.

I sat there near my dad's grave and just daydreamed. I thought about what my life would be if he were still here. I prayed and prayed for Niko to live to see his child grow up unto a young man. My biggest fear is my child losing their father or my child, not living long enough to see his children grow up.

I wept at the thought of both and prayed that I'd never have to know what the experience of losing your child's father feels like at a young age.

Chapter 21
Makenzie Gray

Prayer to my unborn child

I wish mommy were stronger for you. I wish I would have tested my strength and fought harder for you! Mommy was scared, and she didn't feel like she could do it alone. Everything around me was falling apart. The month before I found out you were coming I lost my heart, he passed away, and I couldn't bear to figure out what would life without him be. Mommy wishes she fought for you. I learn to feel you doing something to make me sick so I know your growing. I learn to crave some pasta and when it arrives you tell me you don't want to eat the grease. Mommy loved you. Mommy is so sorry, and now she is so alone in this world she wishes she had you. I pray God grants me peace for my agony. I pray that when you're in heaven you are watching over me. I wish you could come back to me. You were wanted, you were loved. Mommy didn't think she was good enough. I hope to one day get another chance at being a mommy, and I pray you to give them the ropes and tell them not to make mommy too sick and keep me eating my fruit. If you were questioning how I felt when you left, I want you to know mommy loved you.

Damn, why did I listen to him? Why did I let him tell me all this stuff about why I couldn't have my baby. I was so weak I let him pressure me into doing something I didn't want to do to keep his love.

I question that decision every day. I wonder will I be able to have a baby again. Will a man ever love me enough to want me to carry his seeds. So many questions have run through my mind since I have seen the Taylor girl pregnant in person for the first time. It made it real to me that it was someone else he wanted instead to carry his child and he didn't want it to be me. Since the funeral, I have been walking around feeling less than women.

"Man you alright? You have been walking around this bitch like you have seen a ghost for weeks now." Rick says as I get dressed for us to go out for date night. I didn't want to bring that baggage shit into our relationship, but the pain of it all has shown its head.

"I'm alright bae, I'll be alright anyway," I said as I applied my lipgloss in the mirror.

"You think I'm stupid cuh? You need to tell me what the fuck is wrong, nobody wanna go out, and they bitch looking all depressed and shit." He had enough of my moping, and I couldn't blame him. I thought I was doing a better job of not showing how I feel. I sucked.

"I saw Jeremy baby momma, and it brought back everything for me," I say looking in my purse so I won't have to see his reaction when I finally told him what was wrong.

"What is everything that it brought back ?" He questioned nose flaring up like he was trying not to get to upset.

"That I didn't have my baby, not that I wanted a baby by him... but that I wanted my baby and I allowed somebody to push me to do something like that... I feel like a weak ass bitch." I said as moving my hair behind my ear so it wouldn't get stuck to my lipgloss.

He looked at me for a moment, trying to think about what he wanted to say.

"Man, fuck that nigga and that baby cuh, I'll shoot yo club up right now and give you a baby. You want me to?" He says while grabbing me up in his arms like he was ready to eat me up.

"Don't be in here sad about that shit, and I could fix that in one-night girl. Don't tempt me I want your first baby to be mine cuh don't be wishing for another nigga kid!" Girl, niggas love to make a situation about them. Who said I was wishing for another nigga baby I was feeling the pain from not making the decision I wanted to make. But, his little heart is in the right place I guess. He wants me to feel better.

"Come on baby let's go! I'm starving cuh and you ain't cooked shit in days acting all sad and shit." He says waving me towards the front door. But I didn't want to go anywhere for real I just wanted to eat takeout and watch movies.

"Can we stay at home tonight?" His face was priceless. He went from being smiley and happy to turning stone cold. He shut the door marched straight to the room and came out wearing nothing but his red boxer briefs and some socks. He plopped on the couch and turned on the TV.

"Pizza will be here in 69 minutes, I ordered it on my phone... imma starve to death fucking with you." He says still looking at the tv screen never looking my way.

I nodded my head and take off my heels, propping my feet up on the coffee table.

"Nah, fuck that my nigga I need I drink, waiter, can you make me a Henny and Pineapple please." He is so annoying trying to get his dine-in experience at home cause I didn't want to go out to dinner.

"Sure, your majesty! Is there anything else I could get for your while I'm up?" I say sarcastically as I head towards the bar cart in the dining area.

"Yes actually you can, I would like that pussy on a platter as well hot and ready to go." Ha! I cannot stand him. He cracks me up.

"Excuse me, Rick?" I say stopped dead in my tracks as I was making his drink.

"Oh yeah you heard me, bring me my shit, Makenzie." Blowing smoke into the air, if I didn't already mess update night, I would give him hell about smoking in the house. But I'm going to chill cause I been getting on his nerves.

"Here you are my king, Henny on the rocks with a splash of pineapple just as you requested," I say with a curtsy and a wink, grabbing my lipgloss on the table to reapply while sitting back down.

"You forgot one thing Kenz." As he took a sip of his drink and side-eyed me with subduction.

"What may that be?" I say with grin leaning in to lay on his chest.

He grabs me and puts me on his lap facing him. He motions for me to take off my dress and pulls it up and over my head.

"I need all that, I told you to have it ready, didn't I?" He says kissing me on my neck and wrapping his arms around my thighs.

He picked me up and carried me to the bedroom where he laid me down and began to feast on my lady parts. I looked down at him in pure ecstasy. He made his way up my body to my lips and gave me a deep and passionate kiss. With the kiss, I felt him inserting himself into me and exhaling into my mouth with pleasure. We carried out in lovemaking for quite some time even missing two of the pizza delivery man's calls.

Once we were finally were done, he gave the delivery man a call to see if he could double back and drop off the food. I went to the restroom to shower and change, and when I come back into the living room there goes Rick, trying to be funny doing the beat it up dance like he in the Baby Boy movie.

"I did my shit, huh ?" He says with a grin while reaching in for a kiss then licking me all over my face.

"Ughhh Rick, you nasty !" I yell playfully.

"Yeah you did your shit baby, I love you," I say wrapping my arms around him while he eats pizza on the island counter.

"Yeah so give that a month, and we gone see what's cracking." What did he mean to give that a month?

"I excuse me, sir, what are you talking about? Didn't you pull out?" I say, turning him around to face me.

"Nigga hell naw, you been around this bitch depressed over another nigga baby so I figure I'll just give you mine." In a nonchalant tone turning back around to eat his pizza.

"Shit I ain't pulled out in weeks, I knew that you were sad about that bull shit." I ain't never had a nigga try to trap me like this before. He already ran Jeremy back across the country to his daddy house. Rick was certified crazy. But I loved it.

I didn't even know how to respond. I just grabbed my slices of pizza and sat on the couch thinking about what my life has become. I went from dealing with a nigga who only wanted to use me at his connivance me to now having a nigga that's trying to make a family with me. God is answering my prayers as fast they come.

Chapter 22
Kiani Storm

It's that special day, and your girl was finally walking down that aisle. With everything that's been going on lately I thought we would never be getting married, but it's finally happening. We were planning a destination wedding at first but had to kill those plans because Niko on probation and can't travel out of the country yet and it was no was Carter was going to be able to have a real wedding and not have his best friend with him.

We have been planning this wedding for months and it's finally coming all together. This was going to be the wedding of my dreams, and I couldn't wait to see this man at the end of that aisle. My parents weren't too fond of the idea of me dating or marrying Carter after all the drama with his baby momma and the fact that

I can't tell them where he clocks into work every day. They weren't born yesterday, they know I was dating a hot boy. But honestly, their opinions were the last thing on my mind. I was more considered with my girls getting out of there own bull shit to give me a special fucking day.

Since Judith's death, Miranda has been a hot mess. She hasn't even gotten her hair done in weeks. And if you know Miranda her red bob cut is her crown and glory. The new guy she had been dating before Judith's death Liam, has been as supportive as ever trying to make sure she eats and is taking care of herself. But some stuff he has to call in the big dawgs for.

About last week Carissa, Makenzie and I went over to Liam's house to have a sit down with her about how she has been these past couple weeks and ways in which she can take care of herself. When we arrived she was sitting on the couch in one of Liam's basketball shirts and a red fro all over her head like she hasn't attempted to comb it in weeks.

She looked like she was possessed by something just staring blankly at the TV eyes bloodshot red from crying. If I didn't know the situation I woulda thought her ass was gone break into some exorcist shit.

"What the fuck are we suppose to say?" Makenzie whispers to me as we all nervously tiptoe towards the couch.

Liam told us that he doesn't know how much longer he can be in a relationship with someone who is mourning over their ex; which is understandable. She already lost Judith we couldn't have her getting dumped by Liam too, she'll be in somebody's psych ward.

"Hey pooh we came by to see you, you feeling okay?" Carissa says as she sat alongside Miranda.

"Hey," Miranda said in a dry tone while stuffing her face with hot fries watching some court show with people trying to find their baby daddy.

"Alright bitch you need to snap out of it, I'm sick of it! You gotta do something else." Leave it to Makenzie to cuss the girl out while she is mourning.

"Makenzie!" I yell as I rush closer to Miranda's side to try and comfort her.

"We sorry boo, you take your time with this, Nobody can tell you how you should feel," I said while cutting a sharp eye over to Makenzie while she stood there like she didn't think said anything wrong.

"All I'm saying is Miranda when she was alive, and you decided to part ways, you made the best decision for you! She knew you loved her bro you don't need to guilt trip for yall not being together." I hate to say it often, but Makenzie made sense.

"Well... how are you feeling Miranda?" Carissa asked while rubbing her back, trying to give her comfort.

Miranda sat there quietly in a daze for a second, looked at all of us around her and began to weep.

"If we were together, she wouldn't have come to the house drunk! She wouldn't have fallen and hit her head in the shower. If she did I would have at least been able to hear her! She needed me, and I left her !" She stated. She internalized Judith's death. The pain in her voice as she wept for Judith was heartbreaking. We didn't have the words to give to her to make her feel better in this situation. I didn't, at least.

Makenzie however, squatted down to eye level with Miranda, our Miranda chin up to look directly in her eyes and told her with a straight face what she truly needed to hear.

"You cannot blame yourself for Juju being gone Miranda. If you do so, you will never be able to heal. You guys separating was the best thing you did for yourself, and you don't need to regret it now. She knows you loved her, and she wouldn't get right Miranda. You did what was best for yourself. Allow yourself that right to mourn, but give yourself an opportunity to heal." By the end of those words, Miranda was on the floor in Makenzie's arms curled up like a newborn crying.

Carissa and I just wrapped ourselves around them and started a prayer. We sat at Liam's house with Miranda all day, had Makenzie do her hair, we laughed, we cried, we mourned and shared crazy Judith stories, and we did it together.

Now fast forward to my fucking wedding when everything is supposed to be perfect, and it's not. I'm a nervous ass wreck. Everyone around me has been walking on eggshells all damn day, I want my shit to go smooth, and it seems like everything that went wrong throughout the day people were telling me. I didn't understand what I hired a planner for. We already had to push our wedding back due to Judith's death and everyone else's bull shit. We should have just eloped.

"Bishhhh, youz be a married woman now! Somebody about to turn my fav hoe into a housewife!". Makenzie said waddling my direction with a glass a wine in hand. She claims the doctor said she could have a drink a red wine a day and since she hasn't had any she could indulge in one before the wedding today. This nigga Makenzie was a nutcase. She always had a crazy joke explanation for any situation. Glass of champagne in hand I take my last sips before covering my face with my veil. Palms sweating under the tight grip of my pink rose bouquet adorned in gold and pearl jewels. I wore a full lace gown with a long train and some gold glitter jimmy choo pumps. I was so ready to get down that aisle to this man, and I couldn't believe this was finally happening for me.

As I'm walking towards the lobby of the church, my wedding planner comes into the room with a nervous look on her face. I immediately began to cry this day has me on ten with my nerves.

"Oh no darling you will ruin your makeup!" The wedding planner said, pulling her glasses back on her face.

"What's happening why you coming in here?" I say in a troubled tone trying to suck in my tears.

"I want you to relax darling, and I just wanted to give you this gift and letter from Carter before you go down the aisle." With a warm smile, she handed me the note and little box.

I opened the box as all my girls circled me. And it was a charm bracelet with a 100 years sign on it, reminding me of our saying that we were going to be together forever. When I opened the note, it read :

My Stormy,

You the best thing that ever happened to me. You encourage me to be a better man and reach new levels I didn't imagine for myself. Today I want you to relax and know I'm going to be at the end of the aisle waiting for you.

Love Big Daddy Cavi.

A warmness filled my body and any anxiety I had about my wedding day went away. I just wanted to get down that aisle to my man.

"I'm ready, take me to my baby right now," I tell the wedding planner.

Clutching her pearls still in the moment of me reading the letter. She quickly snapped out of it and got on her walkie-talkie to notify her interns to get the groomsman in the lobby to line up with the bridesmaids. My bridesmaids look hella good. She was wearing silky draping gowns that hugged their bodies in all the right places with gold strappy heels. Carissa was my maid of honor, and it was only fitting because her man was the best man. She was my closest friend out of the very tight group, so it was not a hard decision to make.

I hear the music playing and the cooing from the people in the chapel echoing as they watch the bridal party go down the aisle. I waited inside the room until I got a cue from the wedding planner and her interns to proceed towards the lobby.

"Okay beautiful we are ready for you, it's your day sweetie." She says warmly, as they assist me in the lobby holding the train of my dress.

Once we reached the doors of the chapel my stomach began to knot, and my palms began to sweat I couldn't bear to wait any longer to get down the aisle to my man.

Never knew I needed by Neyo began to play in the room of the chapel and my dad grabbed my arm directing me down the aisle.

The chapel was beautiful; pink roses adorned the ground with lit candles creating a lit path in the dim room for me to follow. So many phone lights flashed in my face with the sounds of people being in awe of the moment.

All I saw was Carter standing in front of a pink and white rose wall dressed in a fitted white suite with a clean ass fade he got for the wedding. I coulda licked his damn face.

At that moment as I walked down the aisle to meet him. I saw his big bright smile from ear to ear, and I just knew this was the person God created for me.

Once we reached the end of the aisle my daddy greeted Carter with a homie handshake bringing it in for a hug and whispered something into his ear. Carter nodded at whatever my dad was saying and ended the greeting with a smooth handshake. You would think they were buddies before he and I started dating.

The pastor directed the people in the chapel to sit.

"We father are here today to join these two young people in holy matrimony." Carter grabbed my hand and mouthed "I love You" to me to ease my nerves.

"In my couple of meetings with this young couple, I noticed something special in them. They have the perseverance to push through obstacles in their relationship that most already married couples would have thrown in the towel for... I.. I admire that about this couple they truly love each other, they are careful with their words and how they speak to one another there is just something beautiful and innocent about their love. Let this be a lesson to those of you who want a fairy tale love. It's not going to be a fairy tale all the time but the way you handle the hard times will determine how you celebrate in the good." Claps from the crowd began, and I was just too anxious for this process.

He going into a sermon and I wanna marry my man. I need this to hurry up I told them that I only wanted this part to be like twenty to thirty mins tops. I squeezed Carter's hand, and he looked up at me with a chuckle. He already knew what was going on in my head.

"Carter is now going to read off his vows he wrote for the beautiful Kiani Storm." The pastor says as Niko hands him a small envelope.

"Stormy, you are my best friend, your the most patient and understanding woman I ever had in my life. I've always found it hard to open up to a woman scared of what love could be like, scared to be vulnerable to be hurt by anyone. But you eased that skepticism and a nigga... I mean excuse me y'all." The crowd began to chuckle at home, trying to be proper.

"I ain't never had a woman make me feel the way you make me feel. I thank you so much for loving my son and creating a bond with him. I was apprehensive about that because if y'all know CJ. He doesn't like people." The crowd laughed again in agreement with his statement.

"Stormy you saved my life in more ways than...."

Suddenly the doors of the chapel opened up, and it's Nakea, Faith and Faith's little brother Keith walk into the Chapel. Nakea in an all-black dress with black shades and a black hat and Faith in a white dress showing off what seems to be a baby bump. Keith was wearing a black tux with black shades acting as their security guard for whatever bullshit they had planned. After making such a huge distraction to my wedding.

Nakea says, "Don't mind us we just had to be witness to this shit show y'all calling a wedding" and casually sat down at the last row.

Before I knew it my family was up and ready for whatever was to come. Carissa looked like a zombie trying to figure out how and why Faith has a baby bump and still felt the need to come here starting shit at the wedding unless it was Niko's baby. Makenzie was standing front line with my family moving towards the chicks and Carter was shaking his head in dismay while holding on to CJ as tight as ever.

I can't believe these bitches just crashed my wedding.

To Be Continued...

Credits & Notes from the Author

I would like to thank you, the readers, again for sticking with me and reading my first novel. This is just beginning of FoxxyD Productions so stay tuned...

Be sure to post a picture of you & your book and hashtag **#Foxxydproductions** I wanna know all my people.

Social Media Handles:
Facebook: https://www.facebook.com/foxxydproductions/
Instagram: @__FoxxyD
Twitter: @thefoxxyd

To get updates on new book releases or to join the discussion follow me!

Now, Check out the lives of Faith, Keith, and others in my next book.

The Hood is a Myth

Chapter 1
Irving Kid

"Aye nigga what's the deal?" I heard my young nigga Regis say from the R&R corner store across the street from my people's crib I was posted at. Me and this nigga recently got down at the park a couple weeks ago... it wasn't really shit niggas was just popping it at the mouth, joking on each other, catching friendly fades and the nigga tried to get serious cause I was connecting so I knocked that foo to the ground.

That's my little nigga though, I always looked out for the homie growing up. His mom wasn't shit always had niggas in and out the house beating her ass. So I use to let him spend the night and had moms drop him off at school when she was taking my siblings and all that.

"What you doing over here foo? I thought I'll never see you again after I knocked that ass out." I say jokingly.

"Never bro! We done fought so many times Irv, you just got lucky...plus I'm the little brother nigga you got that." He said laughing while giving me a big brotherly slap on the back.

"Yeah yeah nigga what you about to get into? Smoke up?" I say. That's my way of extending my self so the nigga ain't feeling salty about that old shit.

"Bet bro, link up at around midnight at the stu. You know the one I be going to off Jefferson."

"Alright, little nigga I'll meet you there." Shit has been operating smoothly in the hood lately. Niggas only enemy to worry about right now was the police. Them muthafucka's been so hot the homies been getting snatched up on every block.

The homie Boog just got knocked down by the police over here last week and ever since then, it's been police rolling through on some militant shit. Boog was a real respected dude around here.

He was a young nigga out here on summer break from college. Boog grew up with all of us, but my little nigga was doing shit with himself. He got in school on an academic scholarship no sports bull shit and all that. He was one semester from graduating in the winter and all the homies were gone fly to Washington to support the young. Outta all the dudes the police coulda killed. Niggas that's really out here in the field every day doing bull shit they killed a real good dude.

The front of R&R liquor stood as the cornerstone of Boog's memorial. The news stations have been at that bitch round the clock.

I ain't even gone front, I was ready to get the fuck from over here. If good dudes like Boog getting knocked down who's to know what could happen to a street nigga like me.

"Aye bro I'm about to get outta here, I gotta make some plays before hitting this session with that nigga Regis." I hollered at the homie X2 sitting on the front stoop getting his dreads twisted by one of the homegirls.

X2 was a big ass nigga, that's really how he got his name. He has been wearing size 2 X for as long as anybody can remember. Bro big ass still got bitches though. He always had a bad one rolling with him anytime we had shit going where our ladies could be in attendance. That nigga never had the same bitch with him though.

About six foot four with dreads hanging past his shoulders. The homie was nothing to fuck with. He was loyal without a second thought. That was my brother.

"Yeah I hear you.... watch that nigga bro, he been using his own supply and the nigga been acting weird," X2 says while getting his dreads retwisted on the front porch passing the blunt to his chick for the day, the homegirl Treecey who was twisting his hair.

"I hear you, bro, that little nigga ain't gone try no shit with me ... shit I raised him!" I said hopping in my matte black Camaro.

"Yeah nigga ... you heard me...watch cuh."

I smashed off and headed to my baby's mom's house. Faith was a blood bitch, but you know what they say every crip nigga need right? I fucked around and met her at the takeover. The takeover is a gathering where people show off they whip, bust donuts in the street and show off the hottest shit they just put on their car.

We were on Imperial Hwy and Western Ave and I had just pulled up in the middle of the crowd to bust my shit and there she was. Her and her homegirls standing there. Usually when the cute bitches are at the takeover they usually acting all scared and shit. But not Faith, she walked up to my car and told me she was trying to slide with a nigga.

"You know I need a bad one with me you trying to hop in?" I ain't no ugly so I know she wasn't gone stunt on me.

Niggas had just got a fresh uptown fade. Ears busting with the gold nugget earrings, crispy white tee and a clean gold Rolex on the wrist. She walked up on me switching her hips like that ass on her was weighing her down. Her homegirls yelling telling her not to come my way but she waved them off.

"Open the door... I'm trying to ride."

We've been riding ever since then, that's my ride or die for real.

I ain't gone front though, she been getting on my nerves since she's been pregnant. Always want something to eat then when I get it, she ain't even got a taste for the shit no more or the smell make her stomach hurt. Some weird shit like that. I have been taking care of my baby though I ain't have my pops and I'll be damned if my kid gotta go through what I been through.

I pull up to Faith's apartment door lemonade and fruit bowl in hand to feed this big whiney ass girlfriend of mine.

"Girl yeah, Niko's ass came over last night... bish you know what we did... GURLLL hell naw Irv don't know I'll be dead bitch." I hear her say through the window as I crept through.

She was absolutely right, I was about to kill this bitch.

"Aye what you got cracking in here where I pay the bills at bitch!" I bust in the door to see her in one of my T-shirts waddling in the kitchen with her phone to her head. She was caught red-handed looking like a deer in headlights.

"Girl, let me call you back Irving just walked in the door," she says. Placing the phone down with caution she walks slowly towards me with a look of innocents on her face.

"Baby, you misunderstood what I said... you didn't hear me right." Hands up in the air on some don't shoot shit.

"Naw fuck that cuh I hear what you said, you got a nigga in my house?" I ain't gone lie this really fucked me up. Tears running down my face, nose flared I was ready to blow up.

I grabbed her by her wrist and pinned her against the wall face pressed against hers.

"What did you do! Is this that nigga baby? You been fucking with that nigga the whole time haven't you ?" I screamed, stomach in knots, I felt myself breaking down.

Her pale face red and wet from her sobbing. "Just let me go baby please your scaring me" she pled as she tried to escape the grip of my hands.

"No, Fuck that!" BOOM

I punch the wall a couple of inches from her face. Hole in the wall and my hand bloody. She collapsed into a ball on the ground fearful of what I would do next.

"Leave that girl alone or imma call the police!" I hear Ms.Perkins say in the doorway of the apartment.

"Mind your fucking business Ms.P damn!"

"You see you got these people calling the people on me? I'm outta here bitch, don't call me for shit!"

"What about our baby?" She yelped.

"Man fuck you and that baby, is it even mine? You been fucking that nigga the whole time?" I head towards her direction again.

"I said leave that damn girl alone, gone now boy and go cool off... you young people got my pressure up," Ms. Perkin says pulling on the back of my t-shirt.

"You heard what I said? I'm done with you bitch don't fucking call me no more don't ask me for shit! And I want DNA test cuh" grabbing the keys I headed out the door as Ms.Perkins nosey ass headed to console Faith.

"Where the fuck was you at when she had niggas in my house, Ms. P? You wanna be all in my shit now!"

"Nigga this my house" she getting bold cause this old ass lady in here.

"I pay for everything in this muthafuckin house! When the last time you paid rent in this bitch?" As I headed towards the kitchen.

"Just go Irving!" She pled.

I opened the fridge, took the lid off the trash can and threw everything I saw in the trash.

"I bought this shit, you feeding this nigga my food bitch! Huh?" Row by row I dumped all of the groceries into the trash can. Heart racing I took the trash bag out of the bin. Car keys in hand, I storm out of the door leaving that bitch and Ms.Perkins in the apartment and dump the groceries down the garbage shoot.

Everything I knew as stable in my life just crumbled before my eyes. My bitch ain't for me, my baby might not even be mine. Ain't shit for a nigga to do right now but to get on. I hopped in my whip and smash down Labrea, to keep it a buck I don't even know where I'm going right now. All I know is I need some fucking weed.

My phone rings and it's that nigga Regis.

"What's the deal bro, I'm at the Stu right now if you were trying to pull up early."

Right in time because a nigga really needs a break right about now and I know he got some dro.

"Alright bet, you got some woods bro I'm trying to smoke" I yell through my Bluetooth speaker.

"Yeah nigga, just pull up, I got all that," Regis says, sounding like he was hitting the blunt right now.

"Alright bro, imma come to fuck with you in a min."